Fiona's private pages

robin cruise

D0725916

HARCOURT, INC.

San Diego   New York   London

Printed in the United States of America

Thursday, January 1

It's a brand-new year!

So far so good. Except it's not even lunchtime, so it's hard to tell how today and the rest of the year will turn out. Sam is watching E. T. the Extra-Terrestrial for the third time in a row— "E. T. phone home."

Dad is simmering black-eyed peas, and his whole town house stinks. Why would something as disgusting as weird peas cooked with hunks of ham bring good luck for a whole year? He invited some other reporters from the newspaper and his girlfriend, Sarah, over to watch football this afternoon. Sarah hangs around way too much. Last night, right at midnight, she kissed Dad on the lips and squealed, "Happy New Year, Snuggles!" Snuggles? Pass the barf bag. She vacuumed up the confetti and streamers while Dad and Sam and I twirled sparklers on the balcony. Sarah sure knows how to have fun. Wrong!

I bet this year is going to be OK, because there's good stuff left over from last year:

1. Blanca Lucia Galvez Hidalgo is still my best friend. Mom says she has a sunny personality, which means Blanca always sees the good stuff in everything and everybody. Natalie Maya Winter and Katherine Leigh Larkin are tied for second. I've known Katie way longer, but lately I like Natalie better. That's a long story.

1

2. I live near Wilmington, Delaware, and I'm in sixth grade at Susan B. Anthony Middle School, a.k.a. SBAMS.
3. Miss Dupré is the most awesome teacher ever, and she's going to help my Language Arts class publish a journal for our poems and stories.
4. Sunflowers and daisies are two of my favorite things, but my absolute favorite is penguins. I love everything penguin—penguin pencils, penguin books, penguin pj's! The Adélie is the best of all.
5. Emily Dickinson, Mother Teresa, and Jewel are still my best heroes. But this year I'm trading Shaquille O'Neal in for Mia Hamm. (No offense, Shaq!) Basketball is good, but I love playing soccer—and softball, too.

There's stuff left over from last year that isn't too good:
1. Mom and Dad are still divorced and it's hard having two homes instead of one. Sam still wishes and prays for them to get back together. Sure—when pigs fly. When fishes are wishes. When Saturn rings. Not me. I've finally given up on that idea.
2. Dad has been hanging around with Sarah "Snuggles" Bailey for almost a whole year. Sam plays tricks on her all the time, to get her to give up on Dad. But that obviously hasn't worked yet. Most of the time I ignore her and hope she'll go away. But Sarah is stuck on Dad like a leech.

3. Mrs. Dudley still drives Sam and me around after school most days. She's nice, but I don't need a baby-sitter. Besides, Mrs. Dudley isn't exactly cool, with her googly eyes and her clompy shoes that look like milk cartons.

4. Some things never change, like irritating six-year-old brothers who hide their pet rats in your bed and are always getting in your business. (But even though he's a pest, I'm glad Samuel Miles Jardin is my brother. He's full of tricks and surprises, and he bounces back and forth with me—Sam says we're like Ping-Pong balls—between Mom's and Dad's each week.)

Uh-oh. I smell something burning!

Friday, January 2

Holy smokes!

A year that starts with a fire in the kitchen doesn't seem too lucky. Dad says it was just a tiny fire. He thought that broiling the corn bread to go with his black-eyed peas would crisp it up. Torched it is more like it. Even though Sam and I are supposed to be with Dad until tomorrow afternoon, we decided to come over to Mom's last night. By the time we go back to Dad's on Wednesday, the oven should be fixed and the kitchen will be re-painted. Mom made Dad promise to buy a new fire extinguisher this weekend.

The very first thing this morning, Mom asked Sam and me about our resolutions for the New Year. But Sam and Dad and I didn't get around to making any because of the ruckus with the sprinklers and the fire department. So M-O-M made us choose some things to work on for the next 12 months. I thought Sam would for sure make a resolution involving yo-yos, baseball, magic... or all three. He knows everything about yo-yos, the Phillies, and Merlin. I didn't exactly have a plan, but I told Mom that this year I'm going to try to be a better friend to Blanca, and to Natalie—and to Katie, too, even though sometimes she makes me mad.

Mom said all of us should focus on friendship this year. Oh boy. We couldn't leave the dinner table until we'd each written down five things to describe a True Friend.

Sam wrote (with a lot of help from Mom) that a True Friend:

1. Never farts, burps, or sneezes in your face.
2. Shares all of his good stuff and has way better toys and candy than everybody else does.
3. Says he did all the bad stuff you really did. (Like tying Mindy Rosenbaum's sneakers together during story time.)
4. Barfs when you barf, just to make you feel better.
5. Splits his last piece of sour-apple double-bubble gum with you.

Sam is only $6\frac{1}{2}$, so he doesn't know a whole lot about being a True Friend—but at least he has a few good ideas.

I wrote that a True Friend:

1. <u>Always</u> says nice things about you, agrees with you 100%, and thinks you look perfect.
2. Never gets mad at or disappointed in you—and never keeps you waiting!
3. Keeps your secrets <u>no matter what.</u>
4. Never gossips or passes notes about you.
5. Is exactly like you.

I'm 11½, so I know lots of stuff about friends—almost twice as much as Sam does.

The five things Mom wrote down sound like advice for people who have heart problems. She wrote that a True Friend:

1. <u>Sees</u> you with her heart.
2. <u>Listens</u> to you with her heart.
3. <u>Knows and loves</u> you with her heart.
4. <u>Carries</u> you in her heart.
5. <u>Opens</u> her heart to you.

Mom is 37, so she should know more than twice as much stuff as Sam and me put together. Couldn't she have come up with a few ideas a kid could actually use? She was so excited about Sam and me and her being better friends with everybody this year, she tied our lists together with a red ribbon and put them in a cubby in the rolltop desk. At the end of the year we're supposed to read the lists again and decide whether the things we wrote down were right or wrong—and whether we've been good friends or lousy friends.

Mom already called Dad to tell him about our New Year's resolutions. He said he's going to work on having "more meaningful" friendships this year, too. (I hope meaningful doesn't mean he'll be spending more time with Sarah Bailey.) That's one thing about Mom and Dad: They can turn almost any silly little idea into a BIG project for the whole family—even though they're not married anymore!

I know that True Friend isn't a proper noun, like Girl Scout or Mercedes-Benz, so you don't have to capitalize it. But the idea of a True Friend seems important to me. And besides, this is my journal—so I get to make up the rules.

Monday, January 5

We went back to school today.

Coach Davies says that if I'm serious about soccer, I've got to work extra hard to stay in shape in the off-season. So today after school I started running to build up my stamina. (Stamina is one of our Language Arts vocab words. It's like strength and breathing and the energy it takes to keep going, all mixed together.) I saw Eliot Thomas running near the pond, too. He was bundled up, but he's so tall and stringy—long legs and arms flying—I knew right away it was him.

Eliot sped right past me up the hill to Mom's. I didn't realize until a few weeks ago that he lives just on the other side of the pond. He waved and said, "Hi!" I waved back, but mostly I was just trying to move forward without falling over. I was so tired I could barely breathe. Mom and Sam were pedaling right behind me. Mom rang the bell on her bicycle when Eliot ran by!!!

She is so pathetic sometimes.

Tuesday, January 6

Miss Dupré brought an outrageous cake to class.

She told us that today is the Feast of the Epiphany, and long ago for some cultures it marked the beginning of the carnival season that lasts until Lent each year. The word carnival means to give up meat, but it's really a time for dressing up outrageously, eating, drinking, and partying before everybody starts praying a lot and fasting until Easter. Now carnival is usually celebrated the most during the five or ten days right before Lent starts on Ash Wednesday, the day after Mardi Gras (which means "Fat Tuesday").

Miss Dupré's cake—she called it a king cake—looked like a giant doughnut drizzled with icing and sprinkled with gold, green, and purple sugars. Those are the colors of Mardi Gras: gold for power, green for faith, and purple for justice. Miss Dupré had painted her face those colors, too.

The king cake was yummy, but Joseph Tucker almost choked because he bit into something hard in his slice. He spit out a mouthful of chewed-up cake, and there in the gunk was a tiny plastic Baby Jesus! Miss Dupré put a big crown on Joseph's head.

She said he's the King of Language Arts for the next six weeks because his cake had the Baby Jesus in it.

King Joseph? Sometimes being in Miss Dupré's Language Arts class is like living in another country!

☺ *Thursday, January 8*

Natalie is so tense about her grades.

She called three times after school to ask questions about our math homework. Natalie is convinced she's going to flunk all the tests we have to take next week, when the semester ends. Her mom said that if she doesn't get all Bs, and at least a C in Math, she's going to be in BIG TROUBLE.

After dinner, while Dad and I were doing the dishes—and Sam was playing with his dopey rats, Melville and Emerson—I told Dad that sometimes Natalie is a worrywart. And sometimes she turns small stuff into big stinks. I was going to call Natalie back to tell her to have a more positive attitude instead of fretting so much, but Dad said that I should think about how Natalie is feeling about school and her grades before I give her free advice.

According to D-A-D, trying to fix your friends, or anybody else, can be a tricky business. He says that he and Mom took a wrong turn when they started keeping score against each other—and when they picked away at each other's flaws instead of remembering what had made them fall in love in the first place.

It's easy to remember the things I love about Natalie. The very best thing is that she's the most unusual person I know. Natalie's head is filled with so much music and calligraphy and so many dances and stories, she probably doesn't have room for vocab words and decimals. Dad says there are all different kinds of stars—and maybe Natalie is more of an artist than a math whiz.

Natalie is 110% positive she'll flunk the math test. (She figures she'll get the ten-point bonus question wrong, too.) But I know she can pass it. And I know just how to help her. Sometimes my great ideas surprise even me!

Sunday, January 11

Having Katie help Natalie study for our math test was one of my worst ideas ever.

I like Natalie <u>and</u> I like Katie, at least sometimes, so why don't they get along? I could tell that Katie didn't want to come over to help us, but I told her that something really bad will happen to Natalie if she doesn't bring her grades up. So she finally said OK.

Katie and Natalie and I spread our books and papers all over Mom's kitchen table. Katie is really smart, and she explained everything slowly and clearly. (When Katie explains stuff, she reminds me of Mrs. Hanley, in Social Studies, except Katie doesn't talk through her nose.) The more carefully Katie showed us how to set up each problem so we could work it, step-by-step, the more everything made sense to me—but not to Natalie. She can't remember the order of operations. But it's not all that tricky. If there are brackets or parentheses in a problem, you do whatever is inside them first, then work your way out. After that you multiply or divide in order from left to right, then add or subtract in order from left to right.

Katie tried to be nice and calm, and she kept reminding Natalie to do just one operation at a time. But the harder Natalie tried to figure out each problem, the more confused she got—and the more impatient Katie became. After an hour Natalie and Katie were totally irritated with each other, and I was getting annoyed listening to them bicker. Then all of a sudden Natalie packed up her books and said she had to hurry home to have dinner before her mom left for work. (Mrs. Winter is a nurse, and she's usually on the night shift.) Katie and I finished all of the review problems through chapter 9. She said I'll ace the test, but she's not too sure about Natalie.

Katie thinks Natalie gets tangled up because she doesn't know the difference between moving from left to right and from right to left. At first I thought Katie was saying that to be mean, because she's never liked Natalie. But Katie could be right—maybe Natalie doesn't know the difference.

Thursday, January 15

Tomorrow is Sam's sharing day.

Every first grader in his class gets to share once a month about a hobby or a special person—living, dead, or imaginary.

Sam is sharing his yo-yo collection. He'll do a few easy tricks, too, like the Sleeper, Walk the Dog, or Over the Falls. Sam started yo-yoing when he was five. Dad thinks he should try the Skyrocket tomorrow, but Sam won't do that one. He usually hits himself in the head instead of landing the yo-yo in his pocket.

Sharing is a big deal when you're a little kid. I still remember hauling in my first snow globes to share when I was in kinder-garten, and that was six years ago. I've got 43 now. I'm almost halfway to my goal of 100—for all 50 states and 50 foreign countries. My dad writes for the <u>Philadelphia Inquirer,</u> and he usually brings me back a snow globe when he has to go some-where to research a story. It's weird, but I can remember the exact order in which I got all of my globes: Disneyland, Atlantic City, Chicago, the Vatican, Lake Placid—and on and on, right up to the one Dad brought back a few weeks ago from Tulsa, Oklahoma.

I've got them all memorized, just like the capitals of all 50 states.

Saturday, January 17

Katie and I spent last night at Blanca's.

For as long as I can remember, our parents have called us the Three Musketeers. But lately it's been more like the Two Muske-teers—Blanca and me. All three of us hadn't had a sleepover since I-don't-know-when. Katie is so funny when she isn't show-ing off or bossing everybody around or being grumpy. She knows every single song from Grease, and she does amazing imitations of Olivia Newton-John and John Travolta!

Mr. Hidalgo helped Blanca and Katie and me make a chocolate soufflé. (Mr. Hidalgo is a chef, and he's kind of wild in the kitchen. Melted chocolate and sugar and whipped egg whites were everywhere!) The soufflé was de-lish, but Katie hardly ate two bites. She said she's allergic to chocolate. Since when? For as long as I've known her, Katie has had devil's food cake with fudge frosting and chocolate ice cream for every single birthday. I guess she's just being extra careful about what she eats, because she's skating in some big competition in Philadelphia next month. She worries all the time about getting zits, gaining weight, and how her hair looks. That's ridiculous—Katie Larkin always looks perfect. Sometimes I wish I was even half as smart and pretty and good at everything as Katie is.

We rolled our sleeping bags out in the Hidalgos' sunroom so we could look at the stars. Once we were snuggled in, Katie said, "Let's play Remember When..." (It's a game we made up a long time ago, for car trips.) First Blanca said, "Remember when we got my mom's pinking shears and chopped off each other's hair?" We did that when we were just four years old, and our parents have been nervous about scissors ever since. I said, "Remember when we all got the chicken pox on the very same day?" We were five then, in kindergarten, and all three of us scratched and picked scabs together, and painted each other with calamine lotion.

Katie said, "Remember when the Spit Sisters were born?" I hadn't thought about the Spit Sisters in a long time. Katie was Zinnia Spit, Blanca was Pansy Spit, and I was Daisy Spit. We invented them the summer I turned nine—the summer when Mom and Dad started to…blow up. We were still living in the big house on Orchard Lane, and they'd be smooching one minute and fighting the next. I couldn't figure out what was going on. I just wanted to play with Blanca and Katie, and to ignore my cranky parents.

Dad helped us build a fort in the weeping willow out back, and Blanca, Katie, and I spent most of that summer in the backyard. It was our magic kingdom, and we called it Babaloneya, because Mom used to bring us lemonade and sandwiches—<u>baloney</u> for Blanca and Katie, cucumber and cream cheese for me. (Even though I probably couldn't even spell <u>vegetarian</u> back then, I refused to eat pork or beef or any other red meat.) Katie was the one who first told my mom, "Welcome to Babaloneya!"

One day at the end of that summer, Blanca, Katie, and I had a secret ceremony, and we swore we'd always be true to the Code of Babaloneya: Truth, Honor & Friendship—No Matter What! All three of us spit into one of Mom's old perfume bottles. We shook the spit together and buried the bottle beneath the weeping willow to seal our pact.

And that's when Zinnia, Pansy, and Daisy Spit were born.

Sunday, January 18

I'm still thinking about Babaloneya.

Sometimes I wish I could go back there with Blanca and Katie. Mom and Dad were the only adults ever allowed into our kingdom. We made them our king and queen. Sam was only four, and he used to cry and beg to come up into our fort. But Mom and Dad told him that Babaloneya was a private world, with its own rules. I still have a picture of our fort on my bulletin board. It had a big sign on the front: FOR GRILS ONLY. (We didn't care too much about spelling carefully or proofreading every single word, like Miss Dupré makes us do, when we were nine.)

Last year when John Robert and I used to play checkers and talk, he said it was OK that I didn't like to think a lot about the past. (John Robert is the therapist I talked to when Mom and Dad were getting divorced.) It made me too sad to see pictures of our big house, and even sadder to think about fishing or skating or opening Christmas presents with Mom and Dad and Sam and our old dog, Snippers. John Robert said that sooner or later, re-membering the past would remind me of happy times, too. He was right. (I guess that's why some therapists get paid lots of money—they know stuff.) He also told me that having a journal can link the past, the present, and the future together. He and Mom gave me my first journal more than a year ago, and I've been writing in one ever since! John Robert gave me this journal when he sort of fired me just before Christmas, because my stomach-aches had gone away and I was feeling better about my life.

Being 11 years old is good, but Blanca, Katie, and I will never be nine again, in our own private fort—with stars above us and fireflies below us and feathers in our hair and the smell of honeysuckle covering us like a blanket. And for sure we'll never have my mom and my dad together again, as our queen and king.

☺ *Wednesday, January 21*

This totally stinks!!!

Natalie is transferring to Blessed Sacrament when the semester ends next week. I can't believe it. She's not even Catholic. And until today she never said one thing about changing schools. At first I was mad when Natalie told me the news. She and I are friends, and friends don't hide important stuff from each other. But Natalie thought that if she didn't say anything about changing schools, it wouldn't happen. Her mother has been worried all semester because Natalie is getting mostly Cs, and a D− in math.

I don't know why Mrs. Winter thinks Blessed Sacrament will be better for Natalie. Kelly Grady went there last year, before she switched to SBAMS for seventh grade, and she calls it BS! Kelly says those girls just pretend to pray all day. They memorize old poems and read Latin—and try to make their uniforms look cool.

Natalie hardly spoke ten words the whole way home. Right before we got to our bus stop, she said she hopes we can still be friends. Is Natalie nuts? We both like drawing and doing calligraphy, watching old movies—and playing the piano, even though Natalie is 100 times better than me. Besides, we're still neighbors. I said that of course we'd always be friends, no matter what. But Natalie grabbed her backpack and said, "Sure, Fiona. Whatever."

What a crabby thing to say. A True Friend takes you seriously when you say something important. A True Friend would never say "Whatever" when you tell her you'll always be friends.

Friday, January 23

Today was Natalie's last day at Susan B. Anthony Middle School.

She tried to keep it a secret, except from me, that she's transferring to Blessed Sacrament, but everybody was talking about her all day. Miss Dupré stopped Natalie after class to wish her good luck and to give her a hug. I didn't tell Natalie's news to anybody… except Katie. When Katie called last night to ask about our science homework, she wanted to know why I sounded bummed. I totally forgot that Natalie didn't want me to tell anybody she's transferring. Katie must have blabbed about Natalie to the whole school.

Natalie was supposed to ride home with me to spend the night at Dad's, but she called her mom from the office after school and told her she was going home instead. She said she was shocked because she knew I must have told Katie that she was switching schools. I didn't know what to say, except that Natalie was right— I'd spilled the beans. I apologized over and over, and I tried to explain that I hadn't meant to say anything. The news had just sort of seeped out of me, because I was so sad.

That's when the bus pulled up, and right then Natalie looked at me and shook her head. She said, "Fio, you're my friend. I know you didn't mean to break your promise, and I accept your apology. But right now—right this very minute—I'm mad at you and I want to go home."

She climbed onto the bus, the door banged closed—and there I was, waiting all alone for Mrs. Dudley.

Monday, January 26 ♥

Miss Dupré has been reading to us from <u>Romeo and Juliet.</u>

Joseph asked her why William Shakespeare couldn't just write a story in plain English. Miss Dupré shook her beaded braids and said Shakespeare wrote beautifully <u>in English.</u> (Miss Dupré has 150 braids. She told us her formula last semester: five braids for every year of her life—and I counted and counted and finally figured out that she's 30. She won't be 31 until August. Maybe she'll sprout five new braids!) Then she got all dreamy-looking and turned to Joseph and said:

> *"Two households, both alike in dignity,*
> *In fair Verona, where we lay our scene,*
> *From ancient grudge break to new mutiny,*
> *Where civil blood makes civil hands unclean,*
> *From forth the fatal loins for these two foes*
> *A pair of star-cross'd lovers take their life..."*

<u>Star-crossed</u> means "ill-fated." (I looked it up.) And I think <u>that</u> means lots of bad stuff happens to Romeo and Juliet. Everybody laughed when Mary-Megan Throckmorton asked Miss Dupré what loins are. It's probably against school district policy to say <u>loins</u> in the classroom.

Miss Dupré also recited a part in the play where Romeo tells how much he loves his Juliet. <u>Romeo and Juliet</u> is SO romantic. I bet Simon James thinks so, too. Why didn't I notice him until recently? Simon is REALLY cute. At least <u>I</u> think he is, and Katie does, too, even though she likes Dylan best. Not Blanca—she couldn't care less about Simon or any other boy. Blanca thinks boys are a big stinky bother.

Romeo and Juliet. Dylan and Katie. Simon and Fiona!

Tuesday, January 27

I called Natalie three times tonight to see how she's doing, but she hasn't called back.

She says she's not mad at me anymore for blabbing to Katie, but maybe she _is_ mad and she just won't tell me. It's so weird. Natalie started school yesterday at Blessed Sacrament, and the very same day, a new girl named Mackenzie Swanson transferred to SBAMS. She sits at Natalie's desk in three of my classes <u>and</u> she has Natalie's old locker.

But Mackenzie isn't one bit like Natalie. She's got wavy blond hair, big blue eyes, and perfect pale skin. And unlike Natalie, Mackenzie isn't shy at all. Yesterday, her very first day at SBAMS, she went right up to a bunch of kids and said her family moved here from California because her dad got a mucky-muck job with some big corporation. Mackenzie can't believe how quiet and quaint life in Delaware seems. (<u>Quaint</u> is one of our vocab words, too. It means "old-fashioned," but not necessarily in a good way.) She makes it sound like Wilmington and Los Angeles are on different planets. <u>Mackenzie Swanson.</u> It sounds like the name of a movie star, or somebody on MTV.

Mrs. Howard should be here any minute for my piano lesson. I hope Natalie calls back.

Friday, January 30

Sam tries to make things just the same at Mom's house as at Dad's, even though Mom and Dad are way different.

He loves magnetic letters and numbers, so Mom and Dad both have dozens of them all over their refrigerators. Every morning at breakfast, Sam and Mom or Sam and Dad write a new message on the fridge. When we get to Dad's after school on Wednesdays, Sam heads straight for the kitchen so he can move the letters around on Dad's refrigerator to spell out the message he and Mom had spelled together on Wednesday morning. Today Sam and Dad spelled out: GECKOS RULE! Sam and Dad's messages are always...creative: KILLER BURPS or FARTS HAPPEN!

Sam and Mom's messages are more cozy: LOOK BOTH WAYS or HOLD HANDS!

Monday, February 2

It's Groundhog Day.

I did not see my shadow, so I doubt that Punxsatawney Phil saw his. It was dark and cloudy all day, and freezing. Sam and I went for a walk before it got dark, to scrounge for pinecones for his science project. I saw Eliot chugging up the hill toward Mom's house. I also saw Katie skating on the pond. That's unusual. She works out with her coach four days a week at the university rink, down in Newark. She hardly ever has time to skate on the pond—or to do anything else just for fun. Katie was practicing her split-jump and spin. SHE'S AWESOME!

Katie looked so pretty and so... light and delicate, like a snowflake. She didn't realize that Sam and I were watching. When he whistled at her, Katie stopped skating and plopped right down on the ice. She was still sweaty and out of breath by the time we slid out to the middle of the pond. I asked her over to Mom's for cocoa, but she made a sour-pickle face and said no thanks—she had to get home to do her homework. Mrs. Larkin was waiting in her car, at the edge of the pond. I tried to tell Katie that she's an incredible skater, but she was hurrying and shoving stuff into her duffel. She said she <u>stinks</u> at skating and she'll never be exceptional.

Katie always uses our vocab words instead of talking like a regular kid. She's not the only one who knows <u>exceptional</u> means "superior" or "out of the ordinary"—as in: Sometimes Katie Larkin is an <u>exceptional</u> pain in the butt.

Tuesday, February 3

<u>Today was my worst day ever.</u>

<u>I</u> should transfer to Blessed Sacrament like Natalie—except I'm

afraid of nuns, even though I don't know any. Blessed Sacrament must be better than stinky Susan B. Anthony Middle School.

Mrs. Casey got really mad during Math because some kids were passing notes. She ripped up a bunch and then said, "All right, people! Get ready for a pop quiz." That quiz was super hard. Right in the middle of it, Mrs. Casey called Anne Marie to the front of the room. Anne Marie had a crumpled note in her hand, and Mrs. Casey asked her who the note was for. Anne Marie whispered, "Blanca Hidalgo and Mackenzie Swanson." Then Mrs. Casey told her to read the note out loud. Anne Marie looked right at Mrs. Casey and said, "I prefer not to." But when Mrs. Casey told her she could either read the note or spend a week in Detention for passing it, Anne Marie slowly unfolded the paper.

THE NOTE SAID: "Question: How is Fio like a woodchuck? Answer: She has buckteeth and furry legs." Everybody in the whole class laughed, except Mrs. Casey and Anne Marie and Blanca and Katie—and me. Mrs. Casey's mouth was opening and closing, but she didn't say anything else. She looked like a big old grouper, gulping on the bottom of a boat.

Mrs. Casey asked me to stay after class. She said she was sorry if the note embarrassed me. Duh. She also said she should have looked at the note before she made Anne Marie read it. Double duh. Mrs. Casey wanted to show everybody that passing notes is against the rules. She patted me on the head and said I'm a lovely girl. Sure. Lovely like a bucktoothed rodent.

Mom made me tell her why I was crying when I got off the

bus. Now she's waiting for Mrs. Casey to call back. Mom is really upset with her—and I'm really upset with M-O-M. My legs wouldn't be furry if she'd let me shave them, like just about every other girl in sixth grade. Mom says I'll have plenty of time to shave my legs, if it's important to me, when I'm 13. By then I'll look more like a woolly mammoth than a woodchuck. Mom also says I'm not every other girl—and she's not every other mother. No joke. She's a witch who can't remember what it's like to be a kid.

Who would write something so mean about me in a note to my best friend? And to the new girl, too? Mackenzie Swanson doesn't know anything about me, and now she'll think I'm pathetic.

Wednesday, February 4

Maybe someday, when I'm less like a woodchuck, my life will be totally different.

If only I had a great smile, like Blanca, and blond hair and nice skin, like Katie—then nobody would compare me to a woodchuck. Or if I could play the piano or draw as well as Natalie does, everybody would talk about how artistic I am instead of why I'm so dorky. But I'm no artist, and I've got wild red hair, zillions of freckles, and sensitive skin that burns, blisters, and peels. Not to mention big teeth and furry legs. Maybe instead of being me, I should be somebody else, like...

Savannah Jasmine Jardin

That's a good name for an artist—or a writer. I borrowed Jas-mine from Miss Dupré, but she won't mind. She's got a bunch of names: Miss Jasmine Evangeline Teresa Jefferson Dupré.

Fiona isn't a <u>bad</u> name. But Savannah Jasmine Jardin is way different than Fiona Claire Jardin. Savannah doesn't have hundreds of freckles or a retainer. There's no way S. J. J. would have an annoying little brother who always gets in her business. She probably has an adorable little sister named Susannah, who thinks Savannah is awesome. And she for sure has a mom and dad who are happily married <u>forever.</u>

Savannah's parents are totally cool. Her mom, Miranda, stays home and gardens all day. Her dad, Montana, is a famous jazz saxophonist. And in the summer, when it's really hot and they're not vacationing in France, Savannah and Susannah and their parents sit out on the verandah, fanning themselves. They all wear shimmery white clothes and sip iced tea and talk quietly about important stuff, like new fashions and how to help homeless people. Savannah's life is very calm, and so is she. She's never nervous or forgetful or cranky. And her legs are silky smooth—<u>not</u> furry.

That could be me: Savannah on the verandah with Susannah, Miranda, and Montana. I wonder how much it costs to change your name. I wonder if when you change your name you can also change the stuff that worries you—like the hole in the ozone layer and what you forgot to pack to take to your mom's or dad's house. Or how you're going to look when you get braces in a couple of months.

<u>Who wrote that note?</u>

Thursday, February 5

Mrs. Dudley cut her hair and dyed it red!

It's actually more orange than red, so her head looks like a big pumpkin. Sometimes I wish Sam and I had a college girl or boy to pick us up at school, like Stephanie Flanders does. Sam doesn't mind driving around with Mrs. D., even though her car is a big old clunker that shakes and sputters and conks out all the time. He used to make fun of her, but now he's her biggest fan. Mrs. Dudley can do amazing yo-yo tricks—even Rock the Baby. Besides, she drives fast and sometimes lets Sam honk the horn. (One day she made a rude gesture at some old man who ran a red light!)

Natalie just called. Blessed Sacrament can't be totally terrible, because it's only been a couple of weeks since she transferred and she already has friends, two girls from her ballet class. "Noha did this" and "Judythe said that." Noha and Judythe. Judythe and Noha. Natalie never talks about anything or <u>anybody</u> else anymore.

When she left SBAMS, Natalie thought I'd forget about her. Wrong! It seems like Natalie Maya Winter is the one who's already forgotten about <u>me</u>.

Friday, February 6

I'm glad this week is over.

I bet there's no other kid in Wilmington, Delaware, who looks like a woodchuck. There's probably not another girl in the

United States—or on planet Earth, or even in the whole Milky Way—who looks as much like a woodchuck or a marmot as I do. (<u>Marmot</u> is a much better name for those little rodents than <u>woodchuck.</u> At least <u>marmot</u> is a French word—and I'm half French, on my dad's side, with Irish stuff mixed in from my mom's.) Big teeth and furry legs? It's my parents' fault I've got their bad genes. I for sure have Dad's mouth, big teeth and all.

How fast do braces work? I've had a retainer for almost a year, and next month I'm getting braces. Dr. Randolph, the orthodontist, says I'll probably have to wear them for two or three years. Maybe my life will be as perfect as my teeth when I'm done with braces, just in time for my prom.

Dad and Sarah are playing Twister with Sam. I'm way too old for that goofy game. Thank goodness Blanca should be here any minute to spend the night. Mom is picking the two of us up early tomorrow morning. We're going to Philadelphia to watch Katie skate in the regionals—and we'll get to see Granny Ryan, too.

Saturday, February 7

I guess it wasn't such a great idea to surprise Katie.

It's been two years since I last saw her compete, but it seems like five. I know Katie has a really good coach and she trains all the time, but I still can't believe the things she can do on skates—loops and tucks and camels and spins and axels. Mom says Katie is a great technician. She carves the ice perfectly when she cuts her figures, but I like to watch her fly and spin.

Katie finished sixth, and she had a big smile on her face when the announcer called her name. She was still smiling when she lined up with the other skaters. But when she came off the ice and saw Blanca and Mom and me with her mother, Katie frowned and started to cry. Blanca looked at me, then at Katie. She said, "Way to go, Kalamazoo—sixth is awesome!" But Katie stared straight past Blanca and me. She said, "Sixth stinks. I've practiced for hours almost every day for five months, and I didn't even qualify for the semifinals." Katie started throwing stuff into her duffel. Mrs. Larkin looked like she was going to cry, too. She thanked us for coming and followed Katie into the locker room.

We stopped by Granny Ryan's and took her out for a late lunch at DiNardo's before driving back down to Wilmington. Granny clobbered a whole pile of crabs with a wooden mallet. Claws and guts were flying everywhere. One claw hit a geezer at another table, right on the nose! He must have thought Granny was flirting, because he winked at her.

Monday, February 9

I got a letter from Chloë LaRue Allen, all the way from New Orleans, Louisiana.

Chloë is 13½, and she's the only person I know whose name has an umlaut. (An umlaut is a signal you're supposed to pronounce both vowels when they're right next to each other, so that Chloë rhymes with snowy.) She also has an eight-year-old sister, named Madeline. Their mom and dad are Miss Dupré's friends, and Miss Dupré thought Chloë and I might have some things in common because her parents are getting divorced—maybe.

A few months ago, I let Miss Dupré copy the journal I kept last year, so she could send it to Chloë. That way Chloë could read about how sad and mad and hopeless I felt for a long time when my parents were getting divorced. I think Miss Dupré also wanted Chloë to see that by the end of last year my life didn't seem so horrible—and there was lots of stuff for me to be happy about. At first Chloë refused to even look at my journal, but I guess that when she eventually did read it, she didn't feel quite so alone and scared. She wrote me a letter; I wrote her back—and that's how we turned into pen pals.

Chloë wrote to say that her mom and dad are living together again. Her dad, Johnston Allen, works a lot, like Dad does. (Mr. Allen is a professional photographer. He and Dad should do a story together!) Her mom, Lucinda LaRue Allen, plays fiddle and accordion in a zydeco band, and it sounds like she doesn't make much money. Mostly Chloë and Madeline hang out at their grand-parents' house.

Chloë wishes her mom and dad would stay married. But more than anything, she wants them to stop fighting. I don't know what to tell her. My parents haven't lived together for almost two years. But every once in a while I dream about all of us—Mom and Dad and Sam and me—living back on Orchard Lane. Usually I wake up from those dreams with my heart pounding and my palms sweating, feeling scared instead of happy. Even though sometimes I <u>still</u> get sad that Mom and Dad got divorced—and even though it's hard to have two houses and two different lives—at least they hardly ever fight anymore.

And I almost <u>never</u> get stomachaches like I used to.

Friday, February 13

I got the strangest valentine.

Somebody must have spent a long time making it. The valentine is cut in the shape of a shiny gold star with ten points, and it has a big red heart in the middle. There's *Fiona* on the front, in fancy script outlined with purple glitter. On the back: *"O, she doth teach the torches to burn bright!"* The valentine is so pretty, and it's signed *Romeo*.

Who could it be from? Maybe it's one of Joseph's sick jokes. Or maybe it's from Jamil—he's nice to me and hangs around my locker after lunch. Whoever gave me the valentine is tricky. He must have Language Arts with Miss Dupré, because it has a line from the <u>Romeo and Juliet</u> passage she read to us. And he must also be in my Social Studies class. Mrs. Hanley stopped me after the period ended to say she'd found a folder on her desk with <u>my</u> name on it, and the valentine was inside that folder.

I stuck the whole thing in my Social Studies binder and brought the valentine home, in case it isn't a joke. In case it's from a real boy, like Simon James. I'd pin it up on my bulletin board, but if Sam sees it he'll tease me. So I put it here in my journal instead. *"O, she doth teach the torches to burn bright!"* Maybe Simon James <u>is</u> my Romeo. Simon + Fiona = True Love 4ever?

A girl who gets a romantic valentine from a boy can't be too much like a woodchuck—can she?

Saturday, February 14

What a wild Valentine's Day!

Sam and I were supposed to be at Dad's house, but Dad got stuck in Philadelphia because of the snowstorm and didn't drive home until this morning. Mom made popovers for breakfast. Michael stopped by really early to drop off some drawings. (Michael is an architect, and Mom is a landscape designer. She helps Michael by building tiny models from his plans and designing gardens to go with his houses. Michael is Mom's boss, but later this year the two of them are going to be partners and share all the money and everything.) When Michael smelled the popovers baking, he decided to stay for breakfast. Right when we sat down to eat, Dad rushed into the kitchen. He seemed surprised to see Michael, but they shook hands like they were two business guys at the bank. Then Dad told Sam and me that our valentine was out in his car.

Dad got us a puppy—a chubby black Labrador! He said the puppy's official name is Guillaume Xavier Jardin. (<u>Guillaume</u> is French for "William," and <u>Xavier</u> is my dad's middle name, as in Martin <u>Xavier</u> Jardin.) Guillaume is only eight weeks old. His mother is Guinevere and his father is Launcelot, and lots of his relatives are champions. But Mom doesn't care one bit about champions. She kept yelling at Dad about how hard it is to take care of a puppy. Mom was so mad, she threw a popover at him! He snuck out the back door and drove away fast. Guillaume kept running in circles and peeing in little puddles everywhere—until Michael got down on the kitchen floor, too, stared into his eyes, and calmed him right down.

Mom called Dad and yelled at his message machine. She told him to come over and get "that dog." But Dad hasn't called Mom back, and now Gully—that's what Mom calls him—is asleep on her bed. Mom scrounged around the basement for Snippers's food and water bowls, and she put them by the stove. (Snippers ran away after we moved out of our old house. Sometimes I still think she'll be right there by my bed again in the morning, panting and smiling and waiting patiently for me to wake up.)

Gully is so cool. I can't wait for Blanca Lucia Galvez Hidalgo to meet Guillaume Xavier Jardin!

Monday, February 16

I guess it's not the worst thing that Natalie has to go to Blessed Sacrament.

For the first week or two, it seemed like maybe Natalie had been right to worry about the two of us drifting apart—especially because she was mad about me blabbing to Katie. But Mom and Mrs. Winter made a deal to have Natalie come over to our house after school every Monday and Tuesday. She helps me practice for my piano lesson on Mondays. And on Tuesdays I help her with math. It's like each of us gets a tutor without having to pay for one.

Mr. McCready, my science teacher, would say that Natalie and I have a symbiotic relationship, because we both get something good from each other—like rhinos and oxpeckers do. It almost seems like now I get to see Natalie more than I used to. And it doesn't matter that she's got new friends at school, because I'm the around-the-corner friend she comes home to.

I make Natalie tell me everything she does all day at school. Today she said it's like she's landed on another planet. She's had to learn a bunch of mysterious prayers, and every day she has to study Latin and religious stuff, like about the saints and miracles. I showed Natalie my secret valentine, and she said it's very romantic. She's not convinced it's from Simon, though—because it's shaped like a star instead of a football!

Natalie let me try on her uniform. I love Blessed Sacrament's green-and-navy plaid skirt and the navy cardigan, with those little white ankle socks. I hope it's not a sin to put on that uniform if you don't go to BS!

Thursday, February 19

Blanca was supposed to come home with Mrs. Dudley and me, to spend the night at Dad's.

But she met me at my locker after school to tell me her mom was going to pick her up and take her home instead. That's because Blanca Lucia Galvez Hidalgo started her period today! I've called three times already, but Blanca isn't home yet. She told me she'd noticed a spot of blood on her underpants before P.E. She was going to tell Mrs. Douglas, but Blanca figured she'd just send her to the nurse's office, and then Nurse Burnham would ask lots of questions. So Blanca got one of the pads she's had in her locker since school started, and she figured out what to do with it.

I have pads in my locker, too, and at Mom's house and at Dad's. But I probably won't get my period until I'm at least 20. Mom says that's silly. She got her period when she was $12\frac{1}{2}$, so she thinks I'll probably get mine in the next year or so, too. Oh boy. I don't know which is worse: getting my period or not getting it.

Natalie got her period almost a year ago, which isn't surprising because she'll be 13 on her next birthday. And Katie got her period last fall. But she said that after a few months it went away, which seems weird. I thought that once you get your period, you keep having it until you're about 50, unless you're having a baby.

I did not want to ask Mom about having your period and then not having it.

Saturday, February 21 ☺

Ten Reasons Why Simon Taylor James Is Awesome
By Fiona Claire Jardin

1. No matter how you scramble up Simon's name, it still sounds good: James Simon Taylor. James Taylor

32

Simon. Taylor James Simon. Taylor Simon James.
Simon James Taylor. <u>Simon Taylor James!</u>

2. Simon has a great smile, with big dimples in both cheeks.
3. Simon has thick blond hair, sparkly blue eyes, and freckles peppered across his face.
4. Simon knows <u>everything</u> about football. He could talk about football all day.
5. I'm not 100% sure, but I <u>think</u> Simon has a good sense of humor. He knows lots of knock-knock jokes.
6. Simon has cool clothes and he gets to buy pizza for lunch every single day. He's also the best burper in the whole sixth grade.
7. Simon almost always sits next to me in Math. He must think I'm smart, because lots of days he asks to be in my work group.

I can't think of anything else, but there must be three other reasons why Simon Taylor James is awesome. I'll finish this list when I get to know him better. It's not like Simon and I are boyfriend and girlfriend, but he <u>did</u> trade me a Moon Pie for my granola bar at lunch today. That was sweet, like my valentine.

I've got my shining star right here, and it's all sparkly—as if Simon Taylor James plucked it right out of the sky for me.

Some friend Katie Larkin turned out to be.

Katie is getting a baby brother or sister and she didn't even tell me. When Dad and Sam and I were leaving church, Mrs. Larkin invited me to go shopping with Katie and her at the mall in King of Prussia. Once we got there, Katie's mom wanted to go to Nordstrom, and she gave Katie $10 to buy lunch at the food court. I got two egg rolls, a root beer, and chicken lo mein. Katie kept wandering from one food place to the next, but she didn't buy anything except a Diet Coke.

When we finally sat down to eat, she put two sticks of gum on a paper napkin. Gum and Diet Coke are not lunch. That's what I told Katie. But she said she'd had a pig-out breakfast with her mom and dad before church, so she wasn't hungry. She unwrapped the gum, carefully folded up the foil wrappers, and tore each stick into tiny itsy-bitsy pieces. Then she stuffed all the gum in her mouth while I ate lo mein. Katie refused to have even one bite of egg roll.

At 1:30 we met Mrs. Larkin at the Gap, like we'd planned. She had two HUGE bags from Lulu's. (That's a store for pregnant ladies.) Katie tried to distract me when she saw me staring at the bags and at her mom. But Mrs. Larkin said in her chirpy voice, "Katydid, have you told Fio the good news?" Old Katydid didn't say a word, but Mrs. Larkin did: She's having a baby in September! Katie has always hated being an only child. She should be happy that her parents are finally having a baby. But she didn't seem happy <u>at all</u>. She barely said six words the whole way home.

Michael stopped by this afternoon to drop off some firewood for Mom. He stayed for supper. We always eat early on Sunday nights, and Mom calls the meal supper. That's because we eat comfy food—like chicken and dumplings or macaroni and cheese or clam chowder—instead of a huge dinner.

It seems like Michael has been turning up here a lot on Sunday afternoons. When Sam answered the doorbell and saw it was him, he said, "You again?"

Tuesday, February 24

I don't think Gully is going anywhere!

Mom doesn't threaten to give him back to Dad half as much as she did at first. Last weekend she bought him a crate, 40 pounds of puppy kibble, rawhide bones, a bunch of balls to chase, and a baby quilt to cuddle up with. Gully always cries a little at bedtime when Mom says, "Kennel up!" (He cries even more when she sings to him.) So every night she winds up an alarm clock, wraps it in a flannel pillowcase, and hides it in his crate. The quiet ticktocking is supposed to make a puppy feel calm and cozy.

Michael came over after dinner with a puppy-training book for Mom and some chew toys for Gully. He's got a two-year-old golden retriever named Gladys and an old mutt named Ralph, which is why he knows lots of stuff about dogs. Michael hung a string of bells on the inside knob of the back door so Mom and Sam and I can teach Gully to ring the bells when he needs to go outside to pee or poop. Once Gully is done, we're supposed to bring him back inside, give him lots of loving, and tell him what a brilliant puppy he is. <u>Brilliant?</u> Having a puppy is a lot of work.

Dr. Randolph put weird rubber bands around most of my top teeth today. Having the bands is like practicing for when I get braces in a couple of weeks. Lucky me.

♪ Friday, March 6 ♫

Dad and Sam and I went to the Larkins' for a surprise party. Tomorrow is Mr. Larkin's 40th birthday.

I hadn't been to Katie's since I-don't-know-when. Everything seems nicer and tidier than ever. Her house is like an art gallery— or a squeaky-clean doctor's office. Where do Katie and her parents keep all their stuff? There's no clutter <u>anywhere,</u> and the shiny wood floors are so slick and clean, Katie could skate on them.

The baby isn't due until September, but Mr. and Mrs. Larkin are already turning the guest room into a nursery. That baby is the only thing they talk about. Mrs. Larkin is as peppy as ever and still skinny, too. While she was cutting the birthday cake, Mr. Larkin winked at Katie and told her to go get her flute. Then all three of them played some short piece that sounded a little sad, like it was by Chopin—Mrs. Larkin on piano, Mr. Larkin playing the cello, and Katie with her flute. Katie was so mad that she had to perform with her parents, her face turned as red as a tomato. Even so, she was incredible on the flute.

We couldn't stay long because Sam wanted to hurry over to his friend Caleb's house to spend the night. When we were leaving, Katie was sitting by herself at the kitchen table. There was a big, gooey chocolate puddle on the plate in front of her. I heard Mr. Larkin say, "Eat up, Poky-Pie." But he sounded sort of gruff when he said that Katie had to eat every bite.

On the way over to Caleb's, Sam said he likes our family orchestra way better than the Larkins'—him on kazoo, Dad shaking his tambourine, and me playing electric keyboard!

Saturday, March 7

I'm up to running 2½ miles three times a week.

I usually run one day on the weekend, and on Monday and Wednesday afternoons. (The mornings are still kind of dark.) It's easier to run when I'm at Mom's, because there's not much traffic. Sometimes on Saturday mornings, if Sam is at a friend's house or playing basketball at the Y, Dad and I jog over to the high school to run on the track.

This afternoon when I was running along Cider Mill Road— with Mom and Sam following me on their bikes—I saw Katie up ahead with Janie Parker. Katie started running last summer, and now she runs a lot, usually with Janie. (Janie is a ninth grader, and she's captain of the girls' junior varsity track team at the high school. She lives next door to the Larkins.) They're both fast, and I had to push really hard to catch up. When I asked Katie if she and Janie wanted to cool down with me and then come over to Mom's, she said no—they had seven more miles to run.

Seven more miles? That means they were going to run at least ten miles, if they'd started out from Katie's house. I laughed, but Katie wasn't joking.

Monday, March 9

I don't know what's going on with Katie.

In the middle of Math she passed me a note with my name and Mackenzie's name on it. I hate passing notes, especially ever since Anne Marie got caught with that rotten one about me looking like a woodchuck. Besides, passing notes in Mrs. Casey's class is the worst—she sees everything. I figured the note was important or Katie wouldn't have passed it. But it wasn't important at all. It was really MEAN. Katie had written: "Question: How is Blanca like Mississippi? Answer: She has a wide mouth, big curves, four i's, and lots of s's and p's that sound like a lissssssp! Passsssss it on!!!!"

I didn't pass the note on to Mackenzie. And I didn't pass it back to Katie, either. I wish I hadn't even read it. When the bell rang at the end of Math, I tore it up and threw away the pieces.

I saved Katie a seat on the bus this afternoon, but when I

asked why she would write such a mean thing about Blanca, she just laughed and shrugged. She said the note was a joke. I told Katie she's a joke, and I asked her whatever happened to the Three Musketeers and to Babaloneya and Truth, Honor & Friendship—No Matter What! Katie laughed again and said I'd have more fun and more friends if I didn't take everything so seriously all the time. Katie also said Blanca really does have a wide mouth and big curves, because she's chubby. And she's got four eyes, because she wears glasses. Plus, Blanca does lisp a little—and that is The Truth. Before I could figure out what to say back, Katie went to sit in the front of the bus with Mackenzie.

Blanca just called. I told Mom I'd call her back after I finish my homework. I want to ask Blanca what's going on with Katie, but then I'd have to tell her about the Mississippi note. I'd better just mind my own business.

Friday, March 13

I'm definitely transferring to Blessed Sacrament.

There's NO WAY I'll go back to school on Monday. When we were hanging around at our lockers after the last bell, Mackenzie Swanson called out, "Hey, Fio! Did you lose something?" Then, in front of everybody, she held up a pair of pink underpants! I must have dropped my underwear when I pulled my dirty gym clothes out of my P.E. locker. Everybody was laughing, even Simon James. So I laughed, too, like it was a big joke. I told

Mackenzie that underwear wasn't mine, and I started to walk away. But she said, "Oh really, Fiona? Then how come the tag inside says FIONA CLAIRE JARDIN?" And she turned the underpants inside out to show everybody.

I just stood there, trying hard not to cry. Then Diondre Jones walked right up to Mackenzie and grabbed my underwear. She gave Mackenzie a mean look and growled, "If I was you—and I'm glad I'm not—I'd mind my own business, Macaroni Swanson." Everybody got real quiet. Macaroni?! Then Diondre handed me my underwear and said, "Come on, Fio. Let's go."

Sarah met us at Antonio's for pizza tonight. I told Dad the whole underwear story on the way home, and he laughed. Sam did, too. I'm furious at both of them. Too bad they think my life is such a joke. I tried to call Mom to tell her what happened, but she's not home. Where does she go at night when Sam and I are at Dad's? I bet she's having dinner with Michael again, except it's too late for dinner. I'm mad at Mom, too. It's all her fault for being so organized and fussy about labeling all my stuff.

Diondre Jones is in eighth grade. She's president of the Student Advisory Board and cocaptain of the girls' basketball team. Diondre Jones is one of the coolest SBAMS girls ever. I can't believe that she even knows who I am! Even so, today was a nightmare.

Next time it's Friday the 13th, I'm staying home.

Saturday, March 14

Dad made me go to the zoo this morning with Sam and his little buddy Matt.

I didn't want to go. The zoo gives Mom and me the willies—all those big animals cooped up and pacing around while people take pictures and throw peanuts and popcorn at them. But Dad said I had to go. He figured we could talk privately about Mackenzie and my crummy underwear while Sam and Matt were zooming around.

Dad apologized for laughing last night, but he said he couldn't help it. Waving my underwear around reminded him of pranks he used to play when he was a kid. Showing a girl's underpants to everybody is <u>not</u> a prank. It's a mean, rotten thing to do. Dad asked why Mackenzie would act like that. How should I know? I thought that she liked me. But maybe she doesn't. Or maybe she actually believed that flapping my underwear around was funny.

According to D-A-D, either one or both of those things could be true—or it could be Mackenzie figures that embarrassing me in front of my friends will somehow make her seem cooler. Dad thinks she's jealous of me. I doubt it—Mackenzie is really rich, and lots of the seventh-grade girls think she's awesome. But what if Dad is right? What if she has made a few mistakes just because she's nervous about being the new kid?

Maybe I should give Mackenzie Swanson another chance. I just wish it didn't feel like I was wandering around in the woods, giving poison ivy another chance to get me.

Sunday, March 15

Mom is good at the bait-and-switch trick.

She knows just how to get me excited about something so that whatever is bugging me doesn't seem so bad. I've been working on a sonnet called "Sonnet in 6½B" for my poetry portfolio for Language Arts since December, so this afternoon Mom said I should try to finish it. And that's what I did. The cool and exciting thing about working on a poem—or almost anything you write, except thank-you notes—is that everything else fades away when you're writing. (Pitching is like that, too.) And for a few hours I forgot all about Mackenzie and my pathetic underwear.

My poem is <u>sort of</u> about love, like most sonnets, and it follows the classic form that Miss Dupré said William Shakespeare used: 14 lines, with an <u>abab-cdcd-efef-gg</u> rhyme pattern. The first eight lines are supposed to set the scene, and the last six lines show the poet's feelings. In lots of sonnets the meter is <u>iambic pentameter</u> (ten beats to each line: ta-DA ta-DA ta-DA ta-DA ta-DUM), and even though the meter in mine isn't perfect, it's pretty close.

<u>Sonnet in 6½B</u>
By Fiona Claire Jardin

There's nothing like a brand-new pair of shoes
To set the heart and timid toes a-tapping.
Sandals? Sneakers? However does one choose?
Buckles? Thin straps? Or shiny bows of satin?

Some shoes have tongues and itsy-bitsy eyes,
Yet cannot talk—they're dumb as well as blind.
Some shoes use strings or other fancy ties
To hug and hold the weary soles they find.

Small heels that lift, a daring loop of laces—
Sing praise for shoes no matter what the cost!
They like to dance and take me lots of places—
Stick close to me and guide me when I'm lost!

In closets late at night shoes sing their song
Of all the things they've seen and where they've gone.

I hope Miss Dupré likes "Sonnet in 6½B." But if she asks me to try writing a sestina, I'll just say NO! Sestinas are long and complicated: six six-line stanzas, plus a three-line stanza at the end. You also have to use one of six repeated words, in a specific pattern that I can't figure out, to end each line in each stanza. You have to be a poet <u>and</u> a mathematician to write a sestina. It would be lots easier to play basketball in handcuffs.

I guess I should change the title of my poem to "Sonnet in 7½B," but there's no way I'll admit that's how big my feet are now.

The doorbell just rang and it's—surprise!—Michael. I bet he'll stay for supper.

Monday, March 16

Mom refused to listen when I started complaining about having a stomachache this morning.

She knew I wanted to skip school because of the underwear nightmare, but she said I was making a mountain out of a molehill—and that I'd miss the bus and have to walk the three miles to school if I kept dawdling. Even though I didn't want to see

43

Mackenzie and the other kids, I <u>did</u> want to go to school so I could turn in my sonnet.

I guess Miss Dupré read "Sonnet in 6½B" the very first thing during Language Arts, because right after we'd all written down our vocab words for the week, she called me up to her desk. She laughed and said she loves shoes as much as I do, and she even promised to invite me over someday to check out her closet!

Then Miss Dupré said, "Fio, your wordplay is very clever, and the spirit of the poem is inspired"—like I'd done those things on purpose. When she asked if I would read it to the class, I told her, "No way!" But then she said my poem is really good and I should be proud to share it, so I said OK. Even though I whispered and mumbled, everybody seemed to like "Sonnet in 6½B." Simon said the poem is cool, and Stephanie Flanders, the most popular girl in the whole sixth grade, asked me for a copy.

I'm getting braces tomorrow. I can hardly wait. Wrong!

Tuesday, March 17

Whoever invented braces should be arrested.

It was probably some mean old guy who lost all of his teeth when he was a boy, and so he wanted to torture kids who still had theirs. Dr. Randolph put braces on my top teeth. Whatever I eat gets stuck in the bands and wires, and I can barely chew. I couldn't even gnaw on the green pizza Mom made for dinner to celebrate Saint Patrick's Day. The only things that are easy for me to eat are tomato soup and tapioca. Yuck!

Blanca says my braces are so cool, she wishes she could get bands and wires, too. (Best friends have to say stuff like that, to make each other feel better.) She can have my braces! I wish I had her straight shiny-white teeth—and her big, beautiful smile. Sometimes I wish I was even half as bubbly about everything as Blanca is.

Sam's magnetic message of the day: GULLY O'JARDIN!

Thursday, March 19

My whole mouth hurts from these stupid braces.

Sam has been having a teeth crisis, too. He lost one of his front teeth at Mom's on Tuesday night. When he got up yesterday morning, his bloody tooth was still under his pillow—along with a carrot, a plastic bag of Corn Pops, and 17¢. I think Mom (a.k.a. the Tooth Fairy) was out of money. But Sam thought it was all a bad joke, like the Tooth Fairy and the Easter Bunny had gotten mixed up. He said that because his tooth was still under his pillow, the visit from the mixed-up Tooth Fairy didn't count. He even left the cereal and other stuff—except his tooth—in his bed at Mom's.

Sam told Dad the whole story at dinner last night, then he put his tooth under his pillow again. When Sam got up this morning, the tooth was gone and there were two carrots and $5 under his pillow! He looks cute with a gap in the middle of his big smile, but he wants to know what's going on with the carrots.

$5 for one tooth? Sam had better not tell Mom. She'll say

that's <u>excessive,</u> which means it's way too much moola for one tooth.

Sunday, March 22

It's spring break—no school this week!

Dad is really mad at Mom. I'm not supposed to snoop when they talk about Sam and me. But they were squabbling so loud after Dad dropped us off this morning, I couldn't help hearing them. Even Gully was barking!

Last night Sam told Dad that Michael had used the Vulcan Death Grip on him when Michael ate supper with us last Sunday. Sam had been furious because Gully chewed on one of his stupid yo-yos. When Michael saw Sam kick Gully, he made Sam take a time-out on the couch. I saw the whole thing, and Michael just put his hand gently behind Sam's neck and asked him to calm down. But Sam went ballistic and said he'd call the police to arrest Michael for child abuse. So Michael went to get Mom. He told her what had happened, and he told Sam that if he wants to keep Gully, he's going to have to learn to be patient with him. Sam said, "Yeah, right, Mr. Dog-Man."

Dad told Mom that Michael has no business telling Sam what to do. He said he doesn't want Michael coming over here again—and that Michael had better not touch <u>any</u> of us. DAD SAID HE WANTS MICHAEL STEVENS OUT OF OUR LIVES. That's when Mom snorted and laughed a weird laugh, like a hyena.

Laughing at Dad is <u>never</u> a good idea.

Monday, March 23

Mackenzie Swanson just called and invited <u>me</u> to spend the night tomorrow.

She said to bring a bathing suit, in case we go for a swim in the indoor pool at the country club. And she told me to pack jeans and boots, so we can ride the two ponies she boards at stables near her house. Dad could have been right about Mackenzie. Maybe she feels bad about humiliating me. And if somebody as rich and cool as Mackenzie Swanson would invite me to sleep over, I must be at least a little bit cool, too—even if I did lose my underwear.

I wonder why my stomach feels rocky when I even think about going to Mackenzie's, like it does when I have to get a shot or when I forget where I put something important, like my homework binder or my softball mitt. Probably I'm queasy because that banana I ate after dinner was bruised and mushy.

<u>Eeeeooooh.</u> Just thinking about that rotten banana—or about spending the night at Mackenzie's—makes me want to barf.

Wednesday, March 25

Mom is going to have a cow, but it's her own fault.

Mackenzie and I didn't go to sleep until after midnight last night. Mackenzie Swanson is by far the richest person I've ever known. Her house is incredible. All of the rooms are HUGE, and there are antiques everywhere—not old broken junk, like at

Mom's, but fancy chairs and velvety sofas and shiny wood tables. Mackenzie's mother and father are very elegant, like the furniture. They invited Mackenzie and me into the study to chat with them before dinner. That's what Mrs. Swanson said: "Mackenzie, dear, why don't you bring your little friend along for a chat before dinner? Meet your father and me in the study at six sharp, darling."

So Mackenzie and I sat around in the study, eating peanuts and puckery green olives, and not saying anything while Mr. and Mrs. Swanson sipped martinis. (I've never seen anybody have a martini before, but I know that's what they were drinking, because when Mrs. Swanson's sparkly glass was empty, Mr. Swanson said, "May I refresh your martini, Evelyn?") Then Mrs. Swanson rang a little bell, and Clara, the maid, came in and cleared everything away.

Mr. Swanson said, "Run along now, girls! Enchanted to meet you, Viola." He bowed and winked at me. I felt like I was in a movie, even though Mr. Swanson called me Viola instead of Fiona. I didn't mind. Viola is a good name:

Viola Juliet Jardin

Mackenzie and I had dinner in the kitchen, with her two older brothers, Maxwell and Randall, and Clara-the-Maid. Even though it was just a regular old Wednesday night—not a special occasion—we had shrimp cocktail, spinach ravioli, and crème brûlée! Clara is an amazing cook.

After dinner Mackenzie and I went up to her room. She has

two walk-in closets filled with clothes and shoes, and she has her very own bathroom. Everything is pink and white and perfect. Mackenzie squealed and said she had a great idea—she'd give me a disposable razor so I could shave my legs. I said I'd better not, because Mom would be furious. That's when Mackenzie said, "OK then, Woodchuck!" So I did it.

My legs feel clean and smooth, but I still don't see what the big deal is. It's not like all of a sudden I'm a different girl just because I shaved my legs. Maybe Mom won't even notice. Maybe I'll just wear kneesocks until I'm 13. Or maybe the hair will grow back before Mom realizes that I disobeyed her. It's no big deal. It's no big deal. It's no big deal. Maybe Mom won't ground me for the rest of my life when she finds out.

I wish I hadn't told Mackenzie that I like Simon James so much. And that I think he likes me, too—because of my valentine and because he's tripped me three or four times in the cafeteria line. (Blanca says that tripping me is Simon's way of flirting, but I'm not so sure. He has HUGE feet, so it could be an accident when Simon trips kids right and left, including me.)

Mackenzie promised not to tell anybody that I like Simon.

Saturday, March 28 ☺

I couldn't stand it one more day.

While we were cleaning up after dinner, I told Mom I'd shaved my legs at Mackenzie's house. At first she looked really surprised. Then she looked like she was going to cry. And then she turned red and got totally quiet, so I knew she was super mad. I told her it was all my idea. I also said I'm the only girl I know who doesn't shave her legs—practically the only girl in the whole sixth grade who doesn't. The more I talked, the quieter and redder Mom got. And the more angrily she sloshed suds around the kitchen sink.

After a long time I asked Mom if she was going to say something—like, I'm grounded for the rest of spring break. But she said that my punishment isn't up to her, and her disappointment doesn't have much to do with me shaving my legs. She told me we had an agreement, and because I chose to betray her trust, I'll have to figure out what to do about it. Betrayed Mom's trust? All I did was shave my legs. Besides, we didn't have an agreement—Mom had agreed with herself about my business.

I promised Mom that because I'd disappointed her, I wouldn't make plans for the rest of vacation. She didn't seem too impressed—especially because tomorrow is the last day before school starts again.

I don't know which is worse, making Mom so mad she barely speaks to me or disobeying her and then lying about it.

Sunday, March 29

Mom obviously DOES NOT like Mackenzie Swanson.

That's ridiculous, because Mom doesn't even know Mackenzie. She didn't exactly say anything about her, but I can tell that Mom thinks I wouldn't have shaved my legs if I'd been home instead of at the Swansons'. Why doesn't Mom just get over it? She made me work with her in the garden all morning, even though it was drizzly and cold out. She talked on and on about the choices you make in your life—and about how friends are a big part of who you are.

Mom didn't say anything else for a while. She just kept frowning and digging around in the dirt. Then she put her muddy hand on my chin and made me look her right in the eyes. She said the people you choose to have in your orbit sometimes have enormous power over you. She also said that the older you get, the more important it is to know the difference between friends and acquaintances. According to M-O-M, True Friends are rare and fragile gifts, so you should handle them as delicately as Granny's bone-china teacups.

Mom explained that acquaintances can be nice, but they come and go. And they don't live in your heart like True Friends do. An <u>acquaintance</u> is somebody you know who isn't a really close friend—I looked it up. Maybe it's too soon for me to know if Mackenzie is my friend or just an acquaintance, even though a True Friend probably wouldn't:

1. Embarrass me in front of everybody.
2. Encourage me to do something that would for sure get me in trouble.

The more I get to know Mackenzie, the less I can figure out what she's up to.

Monday, March 30 🎂

Even though Sam and I are at Mom's today, we went out to dinner with Dad.

It's Dad's birthday and he's 40! He acted like turning 40 is a joke, but I'm not sure he thinks it's funny. He said he's going on a strict diet—and this time he means it.

Sam and I made him a birthday card, with a name-poem:

> For Martin, Dazzling Dad
> *Magnificent*
> *Athletic*
> *Revolutionary?*
> *Terrific*
> *Interesting*
> *Necessary!*

I wasn't too sure about Revolutionary—that's why I added the question mark. But Dad really liked that part. I looked it up, and revolutionary means something (or somebody) that can bring about a big change. That's D-A-D for sure.

When Dad dropped us off at Mom's after dinner, Sam showed him today's message on her fridge: AWESOME DAD!

Wednesday, April 1

Bye-bye, Sarah Bailey?

Dad was acting glum during dinner. He didn't even laugh

when all the salt in the shaker poured into his soup because Sam had unscrewed the top. I thought it was another April Fools' joke when Dad said that he and Sarah broke up on Sunday night, but it's no joke. Every trace of her has vanished from Dad's town house—including her toothbrush, and the flowery Martha Stewart apron with matching oven mitts that she always kept on a peg in the kitchen.

Dad and Sarah have been going out for a whole year. And even though Sam and I don't really think she's Dad's type, it's strange to realize that we won't be seeing her anymore, except for at church. Dad says that he's still fond of Sarah and he'll miss her a lot, but they disagreed on some basic issues. He wouldn't say anything else about it, except that it was Sarah's idea to break up—and that she thought it would be too difficult for the two of them to still be friends. I don't get it. Why would two people who had liked each other a lot for a long time not be friends anymore, even if they'd stopped being boyfriend and girlfriend?

I think Dad will be OK. He took Sam and me bowling after dinner, even though it's a school night!

Saturday, April 4

I can't remember the last time I spent the night at Katie's.

Dad and Sam and I saw Katie and Mrs. Larkin at the library, and I said sure when Mrs. Larkin asked if I wanted to have dinner with them. We didn't eat until almost eight o'clock, so I said

OK when Mrs. Larkin asked me to spend the night, even though Katie didn't seem too thrilled.

Katie and I watched <u>Mermaids.</u> I'd never seen it before, but it's Katie's favorite movie ever. That's strange, because it's one of Natalie's favorite movies, too. Why don't two girls who love the same movie at least <u>like</u> each other? But <u>Mermaids</u> may be the only thing that Katie and Natalie agree on. Cher plays a mom named Mrs. Flax. She hauls her two daughters from one town to the next in her junky old car. Mrs. Flax is nice but nutty. For example, she doesn't exactly cook—she just skewers stuff like fruit and marshmallows and pickles on toothpicks. Mrs. Flax is BIG on finger foods!

It makes sense that Natalie likes <u>Mermaids.</u> Her mom even looks like Cher, and Natalie is sort of like Charlotte, the older daughter. Charlotte is a teenager, and she's dreamy, or maybe a little spacey. She has huge eyes and dark, creamy skin, like Natalie does. She's also very serious sometimes, and she thinks a lot about religious stuff. Charlotte is kind of practicing to be a nun, even though she's Jewish. I hope Natalie doesn't turn into a nun just because she's going to Blessed Sacrament, unless she decides she really <u>wants</u> to be a nun.

I've never heard of a nun giving a concert at Carnegie Hall, but maybe one has—or maybe Natalie will be the first to do it.

Everybody in Language Arts had to hand in the last poems for our poetry portfolios.

We're going to spend the next two weeks reviewing the poems and stories and essays we've written all year, and then we'll choose the best ones to publish in our Language Arts journal. Miss Dupré read us a beautiful sonnet. Basically, it's the poet (that would be Shakespeare) telling how his True Love is more beautiful than a summer's day. We started to memorize the poem in class. Then Joseph read this weird thing he wrote called "Guts," about eating a moldy burrito and getting food poisoning. It had lots of barfing and various other bodily functions in it. When Miss Dupré asked Joseph whether he considered his piece to be an essay, a story, or free-style writing, he said, "Excuse me, Miss D., but 'Guts' is a blues poem!"

The poem that Eliot read is really sad and really amazing. It's a sonnet called "Taste Rainbows Singing Soft Lilacs," and it's about his grandmother. She died a few months ago, and you can tell that Eliot misses her a lot. His poem is unusual because it mixes up all five senses—so that seeing, hearing, tasting, smelling, and touching are all jumbled together. I closed my eyes while he read it, and I could imagine his granny and her bright eyes and soft hugs right there in the classroom with us.

I'm pretty sure Miss Dupré liked Eliot's sonnet, even though it made her cry so hard that she had to leave the room.

Wednesday, April 8

Softball practice started tonight.

Dad is traveling a lot to research some big stories for the paper, so he's going to be the assistant instead of the head coach. This season I'm pitching for the Rockets, and Maggie and Blanca are playing, too, even though Blanca doesn't seem too excited about blasting off with us! Alison Lawton's dad is going to be our coach. He knows a lot about baseball and softball, but he doesn't know half as many jokes and cheers and tricks as Dad does. And Dad is the only coach who makes animal hand-signals to tell the batter what to do—a bunny hopping, for a bunt; a bird fluttering, for a full swing; a fox head nodding, to "take," or not swing. Other coaches spit, pull on their ears, or cross their arms to signal the batter. Not Dad. When Dad gives the signals, the batter is usually laughing so hard that she forgets what she's supposed to do!

I just called Blanca to sing "Happy Birthday" again. Mom and Sam and I took her a surprise picnic breakfast this morning. Blanca loved the hair scrunchies and butterfly barrettes I got her—and the cutout paper hearts that Sam and I pinned up all around the Hidalgos' breakfast nook.

Blanca Lucia Galvez Hidalgo is 12 years old. And in just two months, I'll be 12, too!

Saturday, April 11

Today was totally rotten.

Miss Dupré called me at Dad's this morning to invite me to lunch. At first I was excited to go to her apartment. I thought I'd get to see all of her shoes! But it turns out she invited me over to tell me she's moving back to New Orleans. I was so sad and mad, I cried right there in her kitchen, all over the shrimp Creole and "dirty" rice she'd made.

In between crying and blowing my nose, I tried really hard to listen to Miss Dupré. She said that her daddy—that's what she calls her father, "my daddy"—is really sick. He and Miss Dupré's two brothers need her help, so she's going home. We've only got two more months of school. Why can't she at least stay until the end of the year?

Miss Dupré's father must miss her, and he must really need her, too. I hope he gets better. But until she said she was leaving, I didn't realize how much I count on seeing Miss Dupré every day. She's taught me so much about grammar and poetry and how interesting and tricky the English language can be. She's also taught me lots of other great stuff that doesn't have anything to do with Language Arts, or with school. Like how to really open your eyes to see amazing things you'd never noticed before. And how to truly listen to another person, by being right there with her or him. I don't know anybody who's even half as excited about everything—even small stuff, like a butterfly fluttering by—as Miss Dupré is.

Miss Dupré had already packed up half of her apartment. She's driving to New Orleans all by herself, <u>and she's leaving right after school on Monday</u>. The trip is almost 1,200 miles— south through Delaware, Maryland, Virginia, and the Carolinas, then southwest across Georgia, Alabama, Mississippi, and into Louisiana.

Miss Dupré wanted to tell me the news in private because I've been a big help to her in class—and to Chloë LaRue Allen, down in New Orleans. At least Miss Dupré gave me the phone number for her father's house, and she said to call her collect anytime. She also gave me a present to open when I start seventh grade, next fall.

Who cares about seventh grade? Miss Jasmine Evangeline Teresa Jefferson Dupré is the best thing about Susan B. Anthony Middle School, and now I don't know when—or <u>if</u>—I'll ever see her again.

Monday, April 13

Today was like Friday the 13th and April Fool's Day rolled into one, except it was a Monday and it wasn't a joke.

Miss Dupré tried to turn the day into a big party, but her plan didn't work. She made root-beer floats for everybody during Advisory, and we got to have Language Arts in the sunshine. Mr. Winship took his art class outdoors for first period, too, and the two of them had zydeco music blaring and played right along on fiddle and accordion. (I've thought all year that Mr. Winship likes Miss Dupré. I bet his heart is a little broken, too.) But Miss Dupré couldn't fool me, and once she told everybody the news—that it was her last day at SBAMS—her so-called good-bye party felt more like a funeral than a celebration. I've had two days to get used to the idea, but I still don't like it. And everybody else is in shock, even though we all feel bad that Miss Dupré's father is so sick.

Joseph said we should go on strike until Miss Dupré comes back. She must be driving south, maybe through Virginia, this very minute.

Tuesday, April 14

Our new Language Arts teacher is such a loser.

How can anybody be named Melissa Smoot? But that's the new teacher's name. She'd even written it in pink chalk on the blackboard, with a smiley face instead of a dot over the i in Melissa. The very first thing when the bell rang for Advisory, Ms. Smoot made us all sit down and fold our hands on top of our desks. Then she told us to zip up our mouths—we had to pretend we were actually zipping them—while she introduced herself.

Ms. Smoot explained that even though her name is Melissa, her friends call her Missy. She erased Melissa from the blackboard and then wrote Missy, with another smiley face over the i. She just graduated from college in January, and this is her first

59

real job. Ms. Smoot said she has big plans for us for the rest of the year. But she's so boring, I can't remember anything else she said. When the bell rang and we all escaped, she stood at the door, shook hands with everybody, and gave each of us a pencil with a smiley-face eraser. <u>Oh boy.</u>

Miss Dupré is probably in South Carolina by now, or even in Georgia. Why did her father have to get sick? Why can't she come back when he gets better? First, Natalie transfers to Blessed Sacrament, then Miss Dupré moves away. My life is supposed to be getting better and more interesting every day. But without Miss Dupré, SBAMS seems like a big, deep pool of tapioca—heavy and dull and yucky.

Thursday, April 16

40 more days until school gets out.

But I bet Smootie—that's what Joseph calls Ms. Smoot—won't last that long. She was late for school this morning. And by the time the bell rang for Advisory, somebody had dotted the <u>i</u> in <u>Missy Smoot</u> on the blackboard with a skull and crossbones instead of her smiley face. Ms. Smoot looked at the blackboard, then she turned bright red and her mouth started twitching, like she didn't know whether to laugh or cry. She tried to erase her name, but she couldn't pick up the eraser—somebody had superglued it to the ledge of the blackboard. That's when Ms. Smoot <u>did</u> cry, though not for long.

We had to do grammar work sheets for the rest of the period. Ms. Smoot doesn't know too much about grammar. She marked −5 (with a sad face next to it) on my work sheet because, according to her, <u>lunch</u> is the verb in this sentence: "Heidi and Mary ate lunch with Cheri." <u>Lunch</u> is the direct object in that sentence; <u>ate</u> is the verb. <u>Lunch</u> can be a verb, but mostly it's a noun. It can also be part of a prepositional phrase, as in: "Ms. Smoot is out to <u>lunch</u>."

The only thing Missy (rhymes with <u>prissy</u>) Smoot seems to know much about is how to work a computer. She can do almost anything with a mouse and a keyboard.

Saturday, April 18

It's the middle of the night—really, the early part of the morning, 2:30 A.M.

Dad got me up at one o'clock to sit out on the balcony with him. At first I thought he'd gone loco. Who wakes a kid in the middle of the night to watch the stars? But Dad isn't crazy. And most of the time he knows just how to cheer me up.

This whole week was a nightmare. School seems so awful without Miss Dupré, and each hour in Language Arts with Ms. Smoot feels like forever. She cries at least once during almost every class. She cried when Joseph superglued the chalk and the eraser and the wooden pointer to the chalkboard. She cried when somebody wedged all the drawers in her desk shut. And she cried when somebody—Joseph?—mixed up all the names on the seating chart, so she couldn't figure out who was who. Or is it who was <u>whom?</u> Who/whom knows? It's only been four days, but we haven't learned one thing about grammar or poetry or anything else since Miss Dupré left.

When Dad woke me, he said to bundle up for a moonlight picnic. He'd made cocoa and cinnamon toast, and he kept calling me madam and bowing to me, like we were at a fancy restaurant instead of on the balcony. When Dad pointed to the night sky and asked me what I saw, I said, "Nothing special." There were telephone wires, the lights of a plane, some stars, a few clouds, and a shiny splash that might have been Jupiter or the North Star. Then Dad pulled his telescope close and told me to look again. I'd forgotten how amazing the sky looks when you gaze through a telescope. There were zillions of stars shining bright, some in constellations and others glimmering all alone.

Dad scooted his chair next to mine, and then he said he knows that it's been a tough week—and that I must miss Miss Dupré like the Earth would miss the Sun each day. He told me the stars in the sky are like friends: Sometimes you see them and sometimes you don't. But just because you can't see them, it doesn't mean the stars—or your friends—have disappeared. When your friends seem far away, you have to work even harder to find them, and you have to try twice as hard to hold them close.

Dad and I picked a big bright star, and I named it Jasmine, for Miss Dupré. I feel better just knowing that star is up there. Maybe Jasmine Dupré is sitting in the dark, too, holding her father's hand to make him feel better and watching the night sky, all the way down in New Orleans, Louisiana. Maybe she'll see that star shining through the night. And maybe Miss Dupré will imagine it is me, sending her good luck and love all the way from Delaware.

Monday, April 20

Ms. Smoot gave us the dorkiest writing assignment today—and then she made a bunch of us read our papers in class.

We had to write about which animal each of us would choose to be. Joseph wrote about being a python, so he could wrap himself around certain people and squeeze them until their eyeballs popped and their guts gushed out of their bellies. Ms. Smoot said Joseph's essay was vivid, but she gave him a C, anyway. Mackenzie wrote about being a peacock, which makes sense because she always wears flashy clothes and she likes everybody to look at her all the time—especially boys. Ms. Smoot gave Mackenzie an A, for being colorful and original. Barf! Eliot didn't do the assignment right. He wrote this cool essay about being the Moon, but Ms. Smoot gave him a D, for not following instructions.

I wrote about being a penguin. Blanca did, too. At lunch Mackenzie told everybody that Blanca and I wrote about the same thing because we have only one brain between us. Mackenzie said she thought I'd for sure write about being a woodchuck. I was so mad when she said that, I wanted to trip her—or punch her. Instead I said that I think she's more like an elephant than a peacock, because she never forgets anything, especially mean stuff. But Blanca said no, Mackenzie is definitely more like a peacock—she's vain, mean, and loud, and she has a brain the size of a marble! Blanca hardly ever says anything mean about anybody, but Mackenzie deserved it.

I don't really want to be a penguin. I'd rather be a chameleon, so I could blend in with everything and everybody. Sometimes not being noticed can be a good thing. Chameleons and other lizards don't get a lot of glory, but they probably don't get much grief when they goof up, either!

Tuesday, April 21st

I thought Mrs. Howard would forget that I haven't given a piano recital yet.

No such luck. When I finished my lesson tonight, she and Mom agreed that I'm ready to play for an audience. I know it was Mom's idea. She was all excited about her great plan—I can give a recital on Father's Day, to surprise Dad. I didn't even try to argue. When Mom gets an idea, there's nothing anybody can do to make her forget about it. Is there a rule that says every kid who takes piano lessons has to give a recital?

Sam offered to walk Gully after school if I'd try his secret potion. He's always mixing up potions by the bucketful, and most of them are disgusting. This one wasn't too bad. It tasted like grape juice with some peach bubbly water mixed in. Sam won't say what his potions are for. He said the important thing about secret potions is that they're supposed to be <u>secret</u>. Duh!

Saturday, April 25

I'm not too hopeful about the Rockets.

We lost, 2–10, to the Hornets, in the season opener. (Dad says we got stung. Ha-ha.) I'm the starting pitcher, which is OK because Coach Lawton is in charge instead of Dad. (Dad gets really tense when I'm pitching and he's coaching—and he makes <u>me</u> so tense that I pitch moon balls instead of strikes.) I didn't pitch too badly, but the Hornets have lots of good hitters and our outfield STINKS.

Mackenzie Swanson pitches for the Hornets. She used to play softball year-round in Los Angeles. She's the fastest softball pitcher I've ever seen—even if she seems more concerned about her hair looking good than about putting the ball over the plate.

Simon, Luke, Dylan, Jamil, and some other boys came over from the baseball fields to watch our game. I got two singles and a double, a clean line drive past third that brought in our only two runs. Dad said I played a decent game. But we're pretty pathetic. We should be the Duds instead of the Rockets.

Gully is getting so big. He never does his business in the house anymore. He's one smart dog, maybe even brilliant! I wish Sam was as smart as Gully—or at least as easy to train.

Sunday, April 26

Mom and Sam and I went over to Michael's for dinner.

Michael's house is <u>so</u> cool. It's only about 20 minutes from Mom's, up the Concord Pike, but it seems like he lives way out in the country. He's got seven acres of land, with green rolling meadows, a little pond, and a pretty stone wall all around. Michael uses the old barn behind the big stone house for his studio, workshop, and photo lab. It's also got a huge loft, where he goes to meditate every morning. (I had the idea that meditating is like thinking really hard, but Michael says it's more like <u>not thinking</u> at all.)

Michael tried to play catch with Sam before dinner, but Michael isn't too good at baseball. The ball hit him on the nose and knocked his glasses off. So Michael asked Sam to help him behind the barn instead. At first Sam was cranky, but he was happy once he got to split some small logs with a tiny ax.

I guess both Sam and Michael have forgotten the Vulcan Death Grip incident. Sam still doesn't exactly <u>like</u> Michael, but at least he's not rude to him all the time. Michael is OK, but he's supposed to be Mom's boss, <u>not her boyfriend.</u> Sometimes I wonder if she's with him when I call her house and nobody answers. I'd ask her about it, but then she'd give me a big lecture about grown-ups and privacy and relationships and . . . I-don't-know-what.

Later, while Michael and I were making a salad for dinner, I told him that Sam really liked chopping the wood. He smiled and said it took him a long time to understand the wisdom of an old Buddhist saying: "Chop wood, carry water." When I asked what

66

that means, Michael asked <u>me</u> what I thought it might mean. (Sometimes he reminds me of John Robert. They both have more questions about stuff than answers.) "Chop wood, carry water"? I don't have a clue what it means—except it's a good way to keep Sam out of trouble, and a <u>very</u> good way to tire him out.

Sam and Gully slept the whole way home. Mom carried Sam in to bed and I carried Gully.

Tuesday, April 28

Eliot S. Thomas is a genius.

I went out for a run with Gully before school. Now that daylight saving time has started, it gets light a lot earlier, so I can run a couple of miles before breakfast. Eliot was out running, too. We ran more than a mile together. I grumbled about Ms. Smoot most of the way. When I complained it's not fair that just because Miss Dupré left we won't get to publish our poems and stories, Eliot stopped right in the middle of the road. He said, "Fio, if you can't dance, maybe you should whistle instead!" Sometimes Eliot talks in strange riddles, like Michael does—even though they've never met.

We walked the rest of the way home. Eliot asked me what Miss Dupré had been really good at. That's easy—she was the best Language Arts teacher ever, and she was really, really good at making reading and poetry and even grammar seem exciting and interesting. Then Eliot asked what Ms. Smoot is good at. I said I didn't know of anything special, but I bet she'd be a good kindergarten teacher. Eliot said, "Could be, but we don't need Ms. Smoot to teach us the ABCs. We need her to help us use the computers to turn our poems and stories into a book for Miss Dupré!"

Eliot and I talked to Ms. Smoot the very first thing this morning, during Advisory. When we told her our plan, she smiled and said, "Oh, goody!" Everybody gets to pick one piece of writing, and we'll spend part of each Language Arts class illustrating the pieces and putting them together to make the book. Because Eliot and I came up with the idea, Ms. Smoot made us the editors. I'm not too sure what editors do. I think we're in charge of grammar and spelling and punctuation, and which poems or stories go first and last, and making sure everything is tidy and makes sense—and that the words and pictures look good together.

Eliot's uncle is an editor in New York. Eliot says that he goes out to lunch a lot—and worries about the meaning of life and how he's going to pay his bills!

Thursday, April 30

I'm not 100% positive, but I'm pretty sure I have a hair growing in my left armpit.

It's hard to tell about the hair, because I'm sitting in the bathroom sink and trying to look in the mirror at the same time. Sitting in the sink makes it tough to get a good angle on my armpit. Besides, Gully is at the door barking. Writing in this journal while I'm sitting in the sink and Gully is going berserk isn't easy. But my bedroom door doesn't lock, and Sam won't leave me alone. <u>Gully and Sam are so irritating!</u> They don't care one bit about my privacy.

Maybe whatever I saw in the mirror isn't a hair. It could be lint or dirt or an eyelash—or nothing at all. If it <u>is</u> a hair, it's a very small one. Blanca has hairy armpits, and she definitely has breasts. Not me. I asked Mom to buy me a few sports bras last summer, but I don't need to wear a bra—and I usually don't. Sam stole one of my bras a few weeks ago to make a trampoline for Emerson and Melville, his dopey rats. <u>That bra is history.</u>

Mom always tells me that sooner or later I'll get hairy armpits and breasts and a period every month. She says there's no reason to be in a big rush, because I'll have all of those things for the next 50 years—or more. But what if Mom is wrong? What if all the girl stuff that's <u>supposed</u> to happen to me never happens at all?

Friday, May 1

I need to learn how to just say N-O.

Mackenzie asked to borrow my science notes over the weekend, and I said OK. I didn't really want to lend them to her. Mr. McCready says that anybody who needs help should talk with him after class. He doesn't believe in swapping notes, and he docks you ten test points if he catches you lending or borrowing them. But Mackenzie kept begging me to help her. I finally said OK, so she'd quit bugging me. Besides, I've already studied for the test next Tuesday, and Mackenzie promised to return my notes on Monday so I can take one last look.

Why am I nervous about Mackenzie having my notes? Probably because if Mom knew I lent my notes to Mackenzie, she'd have a cow. But it's none of Mom's business. I'm not worried about photosynthesis, so why should she fret?

Sam and Dad's magnetic message of the day: T-REX POWER!

☺ Sunday, May 3

Mom and I had to sign a bunch of papers after we discussed the Family Life Education classes I have to take all week instead of P.E.

Family Life Education actually means talking about S-E-X. The classes sound so stupid: Girls Only, Boy Stuff, Ten Questions Every Kid Wants to Ask, and N-O Spells NO! Mom wants to know what I think about the classes, and what I think about Girl Stuff and Boy Stuff and Girl-and-Boy Stuff. I'm thinking those classes sound really stupid—and that even though she's my mom, I don't feel like talking about any of this with her.

Besides, I know all about S-E-X and how babies happen. A few summers ago Katie found a sex book (with lots of pictures) in her parents' bedroom. One night when Blanca and I spent the night at Katie's, the three of us figured out how everything works—at least I think we did.

Sam is watching <u>The Parent Trap</u> for about the tenth time. I guess if you're six or seven and you still believe your parents will live together happily ever after, that movie doesn't seem so dorky. I'd rather watch <u>Titanic</u> any day. It's more romantic and a lot more realistic.

Monday, May 4

Surprise—Mackenzie Swanson DID NOT return my science notes.

She wasn't one bit sorry she'd left my notes at home. It turns out that Mackenzie forgot all about the test. She was way too busy having a party, <u>without me,</u> to study all weekend. Mackenzie blabbed on and on at lunch about all the kids—Stephanie and Katie and Maggie, plus Jamil and Dylan <u>and Simon</u>—who'd gone to her house to have pizza and watch videos on Saturday night. She spent Saturday afternoon getting ready for her dumb party, and she was too tired yesterday to study.

Mackenzie said my notes are safe on her desk, right where she left them. She promised, again, to give them back tomorrow. <u>Tomorrow?</u> Is Mackenzie an idiot or just pretending to be dense? I reminded her that the test is tomorrow and I'd planned to review one last time tonight. She said, "No sweat—I'll just fax the notes to you after school." When I told Mackenzie that Mom doesn't have a fax machine, she acted like it was my problem, not hers. Diondre Jones was right when she said Mackenzie Swanson is BAD NEWS. And Mom was right about her, too.

Why would Mackenzie have a party when it's not her birthday or some other special occasion? If we're so-called friends, why didn't she invite me? And why was I so D-U-M-B about lending her my science notes?

Wednesday, May 6

Family Life Education is more like Nightmare from Mars.

Thank goodness the classes are separate for girls and boys. Today Mrs. Douglas used this shiny, weird-looking plastic model of a girl's private parts to show how tampons work—and she gave all the girls in class free samples to take home, along with a note for our parents to sign after we'd discussed tampons and pads. Katie called a few minutes ago to say she'd heard that the boys had to watch Coach Richards use a banana to demonstrate how to put on a condom!

I don't know which class was worse, but I can't wait to get back to playing tennis in P.E.

Friday, May 8

This totally stinks.

Mrs. Dudley is here baby-sitting for Sam and me. In three weeks I'll be 12. I'm old enough to take care of Sam and myself without Mrs. Dudley snooping around all the time. Dad says not to think of her as a baby-sitter. He just likes to know that Mrs. Dudley is here to referee and pull Sam and me apart when we tangle.

Dad almost never goes out on the days that Sam and I are at his house. If he wants to do stuff or has to travel for a story he's working on, he usually does it when we're at Mom's. But this morning he told us that his friend Renée had gotten tickets for some big concert tonight at First Union. Renée came by at 5:30, so she and Dad could drive up to Philadelphia. When Sam answered the door for Renée, he yelled to tell Dad that the baby-sitter was here! After Dad introduced Renée, Sam asked him what had happened to Alison and Becky and Sarah—AND TO MOM! Sam told Renée that Dad must be trying to work his way through the entire alphabet of girls he knows, and she's the R-girl.

I wasn't rude, like Sam, even though Renée seems goofy. She brought toy soldiers for Sam and bubble gum for me. I can't chew the gum, because of my braces, but I thanked her, anyway. Not Sam. He handed the toy soldiers right back to Renée and told her that Mom and Dad don't allow us to play with violent war toys!

Sam is in time-out until dinner—no TV, no video games, no nothing, except the Dehyd to English volume of the kids' encyclopedia. At least Sam can learn about Dinosaurs and Dragons and Elephants. (The last time I checked on him, he was reading about Dry Cleaning. BORING!) A couple of months ago Dad and Mom decided that Sam was wasting hours and hours in time-out. That's when they got the idea that he should read the encyclopedia instead of fooling around when he's in trouble.

Sam gets in trouble a lot. He's already on volume 6—just 14 volumes to go!

Sunday, May 10

It's Mother's Day, and Sam and I made breakfast in bed for Mom. It's hard to make a special breakfast for her because:
1. She's always the first one up.
2. Sam and I aren't allowed to use the stove unless there's an adult in the kitchen. (Mom lets me make tea for myself, but that's about it.)

Sam made root-beer floats and I made cheese toast with sliced apples on top. Mom didn't eat too much, but she said it was the best breakfast she's had all year, so far. Sam and I made her a cool card. He drew the pictures and I wrote the name-poem:

For Laurel, Magnificent Mom
Laughing
Amazing
Unusual?
Radiant
Exciting
Loving (and Lovely)!

Mom especially liked the Radiant part—and Sam's drawing of her riding a skateboard for Exciting. And she acted excited about the cellular phone that Dad and Sam and I got for her car, but I'm not too sure she likes it. Anything that makes waves—in the air, on land or sea, or anywhere near her—makes M-O-M nervous!

Dad has <u>lots</u> of gadgets, even lights that go on and off when you clap. Not Mom. She likes candles.

Gully must not have realized that it's Mother's Day. He dug up a bunch of geraniums and chewed on Mom's gardening gloves. By the time she'd cleaned up the backyard and the kitchen, Mom needed a long nap.

Monday, May 11

This is odd.

When Mom went out to get the butter and eggs and yogurt from the milk box this morning, she found a small package wrapped in newspaper. The little card with it had a tiny red heart on the front and was signed *Your Secret Admirer* in fancy computer type. The present was a chocolate-almond bar.

Mom hugged me and thanked me for the candy. I told her it wasn't from me, so then she kissed Sam. But he didn't know anything about the present, either. Sam thought that the candy was for him—from Lucy, or Ling, or one of the other girls who chase him and Matt around the playground with cootie catchers. I doubt it. Any friend of Sam's must know that he hates nuts and bittersweet chocolate. But he does like milk chocolate and caramel and Swedish Fish and Gummi Bears and just about anything else that rots your teeth.

Maybe Simon left the chocolate for <u>me</u>. Maybe he made his mom drive him over late last night just to bring me a surprise.

Maybe Simon James is sweet but too shy to give me candy—or a valentine—in person? Maybe not.

I bet Michael left the chocolate for Mom. She loves almonds, and the darker the chocolate, the more Mom likes it.

Sunday, May 17

Sam and Mom and I went up to Philadelphia to celebrate Mother's Day, again, with Granny Ryan.

Granny's apartment was messy and stinky. I wouldn't be surprised if she has strange stuff growing in her closets, like Sam does for some of his so-called secret potions. Today was warm and sunny, so we'd packed a picnic to have at the riverfront. But by the time we'd aired out Granny's apartment—and hauled away newspapers and garbage, and dusted and polished everything—it was time to go home.

We had to have a really fast picnic on Granny's little balcony, but she didn't mind. She talked on and on about the Foleys and the Mahoneys and everybody else who grew up with her in Connemara, in Ireland. They all used to play in the ruins of a big castle there, and skinny-dip in a lake that Granny says shimmered like diamonds. The way she tells it, growing up in that village was like living in a fairy tale, even though everybody was as poor as dirt.

Granny said that next summer, when I'm 13, she'd take me back to Connemara with her. Mom refuses to go. She says she's had enough of Ireland to last her a lifetime, because Granny and

Pappy used to haul her and Aunt Shaun, Uncle Will, and Aunt Kathleen back there for a month every single summer when they were kids.

I've never been to Ireland, and I can't wait to go—and to France, too, where a few of Dad's relatives still live. But traveling all that way with Granny? I don't know. It would be an adventure for sure, because Granny can barely find her way around her own apartment. I can't imagine wandering around Ireland with her.

Tuesday, May 19

Our book for Miss Dupré is called Taste Rainbows—and it's almost done!

Everybody in Language Arts got to vote on the title. There were only two suggestions in the box, one from me and one from "Anonymous." I thought we should call the book Taste Rainbows, because we decided to put Eliot's sonnet right up front. "Taste Rainbows Singing Sweet Lilacs" is the best piece of writing in the whole book, but it wouldn't be good to end with such a sad poem. Everybody said that "Sonnet in $6\frac{1}{2}$B" should be the last one—because it definitely makes Miss Dupré laugh. The only other suggestion for the title was Guts & Glory: The Secret Life of Jasmine D.! I wonder who made that suggestion.

Ms. Smoot has been great. She worked as hard as the rest of us did on Taste Rainbows. She scanned in Maggie's rainbow painting for the front cover, and she also scanned in photos of everybody for the biographies we wrote to go with our poems and stories. We've learned a lot about computers by working with Ms. Smoot—how to scan pictures and how to use different sizes and styles of type, how to wrap lines of type around art, and how different colors vibrate against or complement each other. Taste Rainbows is beautiful!

Ms. Smoot doesn't know it, but we made two copies of every single page in Miss Dupré's book, plus two covers. Eliot, Veejay, and I are staying after school one afternoon this week to make Ms. Smoot her very own copy of Taste Rainbows, and Mr. Winship, the art teacher, is letting us use his classroom.

Thursday, May 21

Today was a half day at school.

Dad picked Blanca, Maggie, Katie, and me up at 12:30. He took us to Frostee-Freez for lunch. It would have been fun, except Katie was crabby. And she kept telling everybody how many calories were in all the food we ate. Blanca had a cheese dog and a strawberry shake. Katie said that was about 650 calories. Maggie had barbecued chicken strips and a Sprite—1,100 calories, according to K-A-T-I-E. I had a veggie burger, a small order of fries, and a Coke—900 calories. Dad had a double bacon-cheeseburger, a large order of fries, and a chocolate malt—2,000 calories!!!

Katie has gotten so finicky and weird about food. She ordered a grilled chicken sandwich (plain chicken without a bun is not a sandwich) and water—300 calories. She added up everybody's calories while Dad was on the phone with his editor from the newspaper. No wonder Katie is such a whiz in math. It's like she's got a calculator built into her head.

I thought Katie would barf when Dad came back from his phone call with banana splits for everybody. She didn't eat one bite of ice cream—she gave hers to Blanca. Maybe Blanca shouldn't eat quite so much ice cream. No offense, but she is a little chubby. If Katie ate more and Blanca ate less, they'd both be perfect. I'm not sure if I'm chubby or skinny. I'm bigger than Katie is and smaller than Blanca, so I guess I'm medium. Who cares about 900 calories for lunch, anyway?

We went to the park near Dad's town house after lunch. And then we stopped at the Concord Mall before we took everybody home. Natalie and her mom were there, too, and Dad gave us $10 so we could get our pictures taken in one of those jiffy-photo booths while he went to buy a tie. The pictures are so goofy—we look like geeks!

Too bad Katie refused to have her photo taken with us.

Saturday, May 23

This is awesome!

Coach Lawton moved Blanca from center field to catcher. He told Dad that Blanca is a little too dreamy for center field. Blanca does seem surprised when anybody hits the ball out there. But she's not one bit dreamy when she plays catcher. She's totally focused on the ball <u>and on me</u>. Even before she signals me to pitch high or wide or fast or slow, I know just how she wants me to throw the ball. Half the time Blanca doesn't even bother to give me a signal. It's like we can read each other's minds.

Even if Blanca and I are psychic, the Rockets still stink. We lost again—4–7, to the Zephyrs. We haven't won a game all season. <u>Not one!</u> Dad says the Rockets have a lot of unusual challenges, and that's what makes the team so interesting. <u>Interesting?</u> Playing for the Rockets is about as interesting as having the flu.

Just 13 more days until the sixth-grade dance. Maybe I'll get to dance with Simon!

Sunday, May 24

We went to fly kites at Michael's house this afternoon.

Michael had made the kites himself—a dragon for Sam, a butterfly for me, and a bird for Mom. It was a perfect kite-flying kind of day, breezy and sunny. Gladys and Ralph and Gully chased us the whole time.

Mom wanted to call Granny before it got too late, so Sam and Michael and I went down to the pond to skip rocks while Mom and Granny gabbed. Sam asked Michael why he has such a big house. Michael bought the house a long time ago. He figured he'd get married and have a bunch of kids someday. When Sam asked him why he <u>isn't</u> married, Michael shrugged. He forgot about getting married and having kids, I guess. Sam frowned and said Dad is the BEST father in the whole world.

Michael looked right at Sam but didn't say a word. When he whistled for Gladys and Ralph, they came running, with Gully right behind them. Michael smiled and told Sam that he thinks Gladys and Ralph are the best dogs ever, but even though he loves his dogs, they're not the same as a family.

Then Michael threw a stick all the way to the barn and told Sam to go fetch it!

Monday, May 25

Things are not going well for Chloë LaRue Allen.

I got a letter from her and she sounds so sad. Her mom and dad are getting divorced for sure. It made me a little nervous when she wrote a while ago to say her parents were trying to get back together—<u>maybe</u>. Mom and Dad tried that, but the harder they tried to fix things, the more they fought. At least when they gave up on each other, they mostly quit fighting all the time, too.

Chloë and her little sister, Madeline, are living with their grandparents while their mom and dad sell their house and find new places to live. I <u>still</u> don't like to think about selling our house on Orchard Lane and packing up our stuff. Sam was only five then, and he had nightmares about what would happen to the refrigerator and who would oil the squeaky front door. Mom and Dad kept telling Sam not to worry, and I acted like he was being silly. But I worried, too. It's been almost two years since Dad bought his town house and Mom rented the little house on Pond Haven Drive, but sometimes I wonder who's feeding

Mom's rosebushes and trimming Dad's lilacs at our old house. I wonder who's swinging on the tire we forgot to take down from the willow tree when the movers came.

Chloë sent me the cutest penguin pencil. She knows I love penguins. I couldn't think of what to send Chloë back, so I'm trying to write a limerick to cheer her up. I haven't gotten very far: *There once was a cool girl named Chloë...*

What rhymes with Chloë besides snowy? Maybe joey? Or doughy?

> *There once was a cool girl named Chloë,*
> *who hopped and ate leaves like a joey....*

I might write a haiku for her instead. Or maybe I'll just tell her what John Robert used to tell me: Sometimes it's OK to look ahead. Thinking about where you are and where you may be going doesn't mean you'll forget where you've been. It's probably too soon for Chloë to believe that looking back will make her feel happy someday—and maybe sad, too, at the very same time.

Wednesday, May 27

Why doesn't Ms. Smoot mind her own beeswax?

She called Dad to ask if he'd chaperone the dance next Friday. He said sure.

Why doesn't Dad ask permission before he ruins my life? The same goes for Mom, too. I've been waiting and waiting to dance with Simon James, and to find out if he made my valentine—and if he left chocolate for me in Mom's milk box. But now Dad will be at the dance, cracking jokes and acting goofy like he always does.

This is a nightmare.

Saturday, May 30

Mom is furious at Dad!

Mom shouldn't get in everybody's business all the time. She's mad because Sam told her we had sushi last night with Dad and Renée. I'm not sure whether Mom was mad about the sushi or about Renée—or both. But she yelled at Dad because, she says, parasites and other weird things live in raw fish. She asked him how an award-winning journalist could let his very own children eat that stuff. (Except Mom didn't call it stuff. I'd be grounded for a month if I used the word that Mom did.) Dad told Mom to calm down. Mom HATES it when he says that. He backed out the front door like he was being attacked by a swarm of wasps. Sam and I didn't even eat any raw fish. We had cucumber-and-avocado roll. Dad and Renée ate the squid and sea urchin and other slimy food.

We finally won a game today—2–0, against the Firecrackers. I pitched my first no-hitter ever, and Dad went berserk. He says I'm pitching really well. I am getting good snap on the ball, and now I can mix up the pitches—high, low, fast, slow—inside and outside. That's because I pitch almost every game, and I practice for hours and hours most days with Dad, Mom and Sam, or with Blanca.

The interesting thing about softball is that every single play starts with just the pitcher, the catcher, and the batter. Sometimes when I'm pitching—even though I have to know what's going on all around me and what might happen—it's like there are only three people left on Earth: the batter, Blanca, and me. Everything and everybody else fade away when I wind up. I never think about how I look or who's watching me. I just put every bit of energy and concentration I have into putting that ball over the plate.

It's not such a big deal that the Rockets won today. The Firecrackers only had eight players.

Sunday, May 31

I'm going to Argentina with Blanca in August!!!!

I thought something was strange this morning when Mom said Dad was coming over for supper. I can think of only three or four other times that he has eaten with us at Mom's house since they got divorced. Sam was all excited, like it was a big deal that we were all having a meal together. He helped Mom pick flowers, and he even set the table. (Gully wasn't excited, though. He growled and barked when Dad came in the door. I've never once heard Gully growl before.) But it wasn't a big deal at all. Dad and Mom just wanted to give me an early birthday present. Tomorrow is the real day, but Dad has to go up to Boston late tonight. He's interviewing some famous scientist at the Massachusetts Institute of Technology, and he'll be gone until Friday morning.

Dad grilled halibut, and Mom sliced tomatoes from the garden and cooked string beans and new potatoes with butter and parsley—everything I like. Plus we ate in the dining room instead of in the kitchen. So I definitely should have known they were up to something. After Mom cleared the table, Dad came out of the kitchen carrying a huge carrot cake with sparklers sputtering on top. He sang "Bon Anniversaire" ("Happy Birthday" in French), and then the three of them sang again in English!

Mom handed me a pretty package all wrapped up in purple and turquoise, my favorite colors. Inside was a big, heavy book about Argentina. It's a perfectly nice book, with lots of great pictures and maps and charts. But I guess I didn't seem too thrilled. Dad said what he always does when I look disappointed because he or Mom has bought me another book: "You can't judge a book by its cover." Then he said, "Find the adventure, Fio-bean!"

So I opened the book again and found an envelope. There was a plane ticket inside, round-trip from Philadelphia to Chicago to Buenos Aires and back. That ticket has my name on it!

〈 Monday, June 1 〉

So far being 12 is pretty good.

Mom made waffles with fresh strawberries and whipped cream for breakfast, like she always does on my birthday. She even put Tootsie Rolls on top, like Dad does for special occasions! Even though today is my actual birthday, I'm not having my party until Saturday. Mom hates slumber parties, but she's letting me have Blanca, Natalie, Katie, Anne Marie, Maggie, Frankie, and Dawn sleep over. (Mom thinks slumber parties should be called <u>un</u>slumber <u>un</u>parties, because nobody sleeps at them and they're no fun for the parents who end up with cranky kids the next day.) She made me promise that everybody will be ready for bed by 11 o'clock and asleep by midnight. How did Mom get so wild—ha!

I got to open a bunch of presents at breakfast, including two Dad brought over last night. He got me a new softball mitt, a Wilson—and it's a beauty! He also gave me big black batting gloves that are scary looking. Sam had wrapped up one of his old yo-yos. Granny sent a book about Ireland and a plane ticket IOU, for when she takes me to Connemara next summer. And Michael got me a pretty little kaleidoscope. The message on the card that he made is so cool: "There are lots of wonderful ways to see the world <u>if</u> you open your eyes. Happy birthday, Fiona."

I saved Mom's present for last. The wrapping was so pretty, I almost didn't want to open the gift. Mom could go into business wrapping presents. She always uses fancy ribbons and twine and dried flowers and tiny bells and feathers and other good stuff. Mom says the package is part of the gift, so the <u>outside</u> should be as surprising and thoughtful as the present <u>inside.</u> Pretty wrapping is nice, but the gift is for sure the best part.

I can't believe it! Mom gave me a razor. It's silver, with *FCJ* engraved on it in fancy cursive. She hugged me and said that sometimes it's hard for her to admit I'm growing up. She gave me shaving gel and body lotion, too—and a rubber ducky to keep me company in the tub! The razor is great, but shaving your legs seems like a nuisance. Why bother? Besides, even though the hair has grown back on my legs, you can barely see it.

Maybe I'll just wait until next year, when I'm 13, to shave. Or maybe I won't shave my legs again at all.

Friday, June 5

D-I-S-A-S-T-E-R.

I shouldn't have gone to that dumb sixth-grade dance. And Ms. Smoot shouldn't have asked my dad to chaperone. For sure I never should have told Mackenzie Swanson how much I like Simon James, <u>even though I don't anymore.</u>

Mackenzie and Simon came to the dance TOGETHER. They danced every single dance, until the very end. For most of the night, Blanca sat with me in the hall in front of the gym. There was no way I was going to go into the gym so Mackenzie could embarrass me again. Blanca couldn't have cared less about the dance. She still thinks boys are useless, and she said I shouldn't waste my time and energy on Simon James <u>or</u> on Mackenzie Swanson. Even from the front hall I could see them dancing—not that I was watching. And Dad and Ms. Smoot danced together, too. THEY WERE DOING THE MACARENA!

At 9:45, just before the dance ended, Mackenzie and Simon came out in the hall <u>holding hands.</u> I wished I could have melted right into the floor. I couldn't believe Mackenzie would humiliate me like that after I'd told her in private how much I liked Simon.

But Mackenzie dragged him right up to me, winked, and said loudly, so everybody could hear, "Fiona, here's your sweetie. Want to dance with him?"

I was about to tell them both to take a leap, when Eliot walked up and said I'd promised <u>him</u> the last dance. Is Eliot from Mars? I never promised to dance with him, but Blanca gave me a little shove, so I went into the gym, anyway.

Eliot S. Thomas is an excellent dancer!

Sunday, June 7

I didn't want to have my birthday sleepover last night, but I'm glad I did.

I was so mad and sad all day yesterday, after the dance nightmare, that I didn't want to see <u>anybody.</u> But Mom wouldn't let me cancel the party. She said that having friends around when you're sad is just as important as having them around when you're happy. Mom was right, like she almost always is. Is there a rule that says mothers have to be right 97% of the time?

Maggie says Mackenzie Swanson isn't the sharpest blade in the drawer. She also says Simon James is pond scum! I thought Simon was going to be my True Love 4ever, or at least for the dance. That valentine I've been saving in this journal must have been a mean joke from somebody. I started to rip it up, but it's so pretty I couldn't do it. If Simon didn't make it, who did?

My friends chipped in and got me the coolest karaoke machine! We stayed up past midnight, singing and dancing to a bunch of Mom's oldies. We poufed up our hair and dressed in her shimmery old cocktail dresses. She sang and danced with us, too.

It's a good thing that Sam was spending the night at Matt's— he would have freaked.

Monday, June 8

Ten Reasons Why
Simon Taylor James Is Pond Scum
By Fiona Claire Jardin

1. Simon Taylor James is a dumb name. It's stupid to have three first names for your official name, like Billy Joe Bob.
2. Simon should brush his teeth more often. They're green and fuzzy looking.
3. Simon has more zits than freckles.
4. Simon never talks about anything except football, football, and football.
5. Simon's sense of humor is limited to knock-knock jokes.
6. Simon should be more careful about his diet. He seems to have bad digestive problems.
7. Simon cheats in Math.
8. Simon has killer B.O.
9. Simon's feet are ten times bigger than his brain.
10. Simon looks like a robot when he dances.

That's already ten reasons. There are <u>lots</u> more.

Whoever he or she is, the so-called Secret Admirer isn't very elegant. Mom found a little packet of bath salts in the milk box this morning, all wrapped up in yesterday's funny pages and tied with a red shoelace. Mom said the bath salts must be for me, but I don't want them.

<u>They're definitely not from Simon James.</u>

Tuesday, June 9

Dad came over for dinner again.

Sam was all excited, like it was another big deal, which it wasn't. Mom and Dad just wanted to figure out the plan for when school gets out next week. This summer will be way better than last summer for Sam and me. For one thing, Blanca and I are going to Argentina in August! And for another, she and I get to help with the little kids at YMCA camp two afternoons a week until we leave. Sam is going to Y camp every day for six whole weeks. I'd be bored, but Sam loves all that stuff—archery and badminton and swimming and crafts, building rockets and model airplanes, and doing silly skits.

Mrs. Dudley is taking seven weeks off this summer—all of July and the two-and-a-half weeks I'll be in Argentina during August. Sometimes Mrs. D. is so surprising. She's going on an African safari next month! Mom is staying home on Tuesdays, and I get to do stuff with Natalie and Mrs. Winter while Mom is at work on Mondays and Wednesdays. I'm taking Spanish lessons on Thursday mornings, and Blanca and I are helping on Fridays at the restaurant where her dad is the chef.

Natalie and I agreed to baby-sit the Alexander twins for three hours every Wednesday morning, and Mrs. Alexander is going to pay us $6 each. Blanca and I will get $10 every Friday from Mr. Hidalgo. That's $16 a week for baby-sitting and helping Blanca's dad, plus $8 from both Mom and Dad for doing my chores. $32 a week? I'll be rich by the time Blanca and I go to Argentina!

Dad is taking Sam and me to Martha's Vineyard for ten days in July. We're staying at his friend Paul's summerhouse, in a little town called Gay Head. It's the first real vacation we've taken (except going to the Jersey Shore for a few days to see Mama and Papa Jardin and Dad's other relatives) since we went to Cape Cod three years ago, when Mom and Dad were still married. Sam doesn't remember the beach house we stayed at, but I do. And I remember Mom and Dad holding hands when the four of us watched the sunset together every single night.

Sam's magnetic letters on Mom's fridge spell: IMAGINE TURTLES!

Wednesday, June 10

We sent Taste Rainbows to Miss Dupré today.

It's kind of scary to finish a book and then let it go, but like Ms. Smoot says, "Goody! What's done is done!" We called FedEx during Advisory, and some guy came to pick up the package. He said that Miss Dupré will have her book by ten o'clock tomorrow morning, guaranteed.

I hope Miss Dupré likes Taste Rainbows even half as much as Ms. Smoot does. She cried at the end of class (this time they were happy tears) and gave each of us a smiley-face cupcake. It turns out that Ms. Smoot is coming back to SBAMS next year to run the computer lab. She wants to start a computer club, too—and Joseph volunteered to help her! Maybe this summer Ms. Smoot will get beyond smiley faces and realize that Roxy or NFL stickers are way cooler for 12-year-olds.

And maybe next year Miss Dupré will come back to teach seventh-grade Language Arts....

Is Thursday, June 11?!

SCHOOL IS OUT—HI-HO SEVENTH GRADE!

Blanca is spending the night. Dad made something called bife a caballo for dinner. He's going way overboard about Argentina. Bife a caballo is cowboy-style steak, with a fried egg on top. That's how some people eat steak in Argentina. They eat lots of beef there because of all the cattle ranches. I hope they have plenty of peanut butter and cream cheese, too, for vegetarians like me. I told Dad to cook my egg over easy—and to hold the bife!

Dad and Blanca tried to teach me some Spanish. (My lessons don't start until a week from today.) Dad knows about as much Spanish as the Man in the Moon. He said there are only three essential things to know how to say in any language:

    1. "Where is the bathroom?" That's easy. Even I can
       say, "¿Dónde está el baño?"

2. "You have very pretty eyes." "<u>Tienes ojos muy</u>
   <u>bonitos.</u>" Why would anybody need to know how
   to say <u>that</u>?
3. "Please pass the potatoes." That should be "<u>Pásame</u>
   <u>las papas por favor.</u>" But Dad said, "<u>Pásame el</u>
   <u>cuaderno por favor,</u>" which means "Pass me the
   notebook, please"!

Blanca laughed so hard at that one, she spit milk all over the
table. Dad should stick to cooking macaroni and cheese and
speaking English. He sure knows how to turn an adventure into
a serious pain in the butt. Maybe <u>he</u> should go to Argentina with
Blanca instead of me.

Mom is just as bad. When Sam and I play Scrabble with her,
she gives me a triple word-score for every Spanish word I make.
How many points do I get for L-O-C-O?

Friday, June 12

Sam and I made a deal with Dad.

He's going to keep the women he dates private, instead of trying to make them chummy with Sam and me. I feel bad for
Renée. Dad had to carry her from the bowling alley out to his car,
but we're pretty sure her foot isn't broken. If her skirt hadn't
been so short and so tight, she could have bent down a little
lower to roll the ball—and then it wouldn't have dropped on her
foot. I've never seen anybody roll so many gutter balls, and most

of the balls that didn't go in the gutter stopped dead, halfway down the lane.

Mom is an awesome bowler. Half the time she sl-i-i-i-des down the lane along with the ball. She could give Renée a few tips!

Sunday, June 14

I'm worried that Mom and Dad are spending too much money for me to go to Argentina with Blanca.

Dad told me I have to research our trip from A to Z, so that's what I've been doing. Today I called the airlines. It's probably costing Mom and Dad about $1,800 to send me to Argentina and back—and that's just the airfare. It's almost 700 miles from Philadelphia to Chicago, and it's going to take Blanca and me 2 hours and 18 minutes to get there. We're flying that far all by ourselves. Then we have to wait a few hours with her aunt Isabel and her cousin Alejandro. They're flying to Chicago from Los Angeles, and then we're all going on together to Buenos Aires. (I've seen pictures of Alejandro, and he's totally cute! He's 14, and Blanca says he's really good at soccer.)

It's 5,602 miles from Chicago to Buenos Aires, and the flight takes 10 hours and 55 minutes—we'll arrive the morning after we leave Philadelphia. Once we land in Buenos Aires, it's a seven-hour drive to the village in the foothills of the Andes where Blanca's mom grew up. Mrs. Hidalgo is a doctor, and for two months every summer, she helps at a clinic in that little village. Blanca says I'm going to love seeing the gauchos on the pampas and eating empanadas and dulce de leche. But I don't care too much about cowboys riding around on the plains or about eating turnovers and slimy custard.

My parents are sending me more than 6,000 miles from home for two-and-a-half weeks. I should be really excited. So why does my stomach flop every time I think about the trip? August is the middle of winter in South America. It's freezing there, and dangerous to drive in the mountains. I could be here instead, helping at the Y and hanging out at the pool with Maggie and Anne Marie and maybe Katie, when she's not being a grouch. I could be gardening with my mom, driving Dad's golf cart, making potions with Sam—and running with Eliot some days.

While we were doing the dishes, I told Mom I'm worried that she and Dad are spending too much money on me. But she reminded me of something John Robert said over and over: It's not my job or Sam's to worry about money. Mom asked if I'm scared about the trip. Scared? I can hardly wait to go to Argentina with Blanca. Maybe if I say that a lot it will be true: I can't wait to go to Argentina with Blanca! I can't wait to go to Argentina with Blanca!

Sometimes it's like Mom can see right through me.

Wednesday, June 17

I'm sick of Argentina—no offense to Blanca and the rest of the Hidalgos.

Now Dad and somebody named Liza are taking tango lessons on Tuesday nights, when Sam and I are at Mom's. (Sam wants to know what happened to Renée. He was just starting to like her!) Dad is now an expert on the tango, along with just about everything else. And every Wednesday after dinner, he gives Sam and me a tango lesson, too. Who cares that the tango was invented a hundred years ago in Buenos Aires? Who cares that it's a romantic dance that mixes a bunch of cultures together? For a long time, people thought the tango was nasty. I think it's nasty, too— and I've got bruises on my ankles and shins to prove it.

Gully has gotten ENORMOUS! I take him running with me most mornings when I'm at Mom's. I'd much rather have him huffing beside me than Mom and Sam pedaling behind me. Almost every day, Eliot catches up with us. He's a great runner, and he makes running seem almost easy. He's got such a long, strong stride, and he gives me good tips—shoulders back, chin up, knees high, lengthen my stride. And he knows lots of jokes! We had so much fun just talking and running this morning, I asked him to come to my recital on Sunday. What if I mess up?

Natalie and I played the piano for a couple of hours while we were watching the Alexander twins this morning. She's teaching me this amazing piece for two people to play together.

Natalie makes playing the piano seem almost easy!

Friday, June 19

Sam and Dad and I played the longest game of Monopoly after dinner.

Sam fell asleep on the floor right after he landed on Park

Place and then went bankrupt. Dad owned Boardwalk and Park Place, and he'd loaded them both up with hotels, like he always does. I said it was mean to make Sam go broke. But Dad laughed and reminded me that Monopoly is only a game and that it's good to have a competitive spirit. Then he asked me why I'd seemed so quiet and thoughtful all night.

I didn't want to tell him that I've been thinking a lot about Argentina—and worrying about getting homesick. So instead I asked Dad to tell me about the most exciting adventure he's ever had. He said it might have been the time he was nine and got lost with Uncle Harvey in Paris. Or maybe when he and his friend Paul went white-water rafting in Colorado when they were 16. But then Dad smiled and said that his biggest adventure so far was living in France, marrying Mom, and having a family.

When Dad asked if I'm getting excited about my big adventure, I said sure. And I am—sort of. Ever since we were five, Blanca and I have dreamed of going to Argentina together. And now, in 56 days, I'm going all the way to South America for two-and-a-half weeks. Maybe my stomach is queasy because I'm so excited. Or because we're playing the Cyclones tomorrow. Or maybe I'm nervous because it's only nine days until my piano recital.

Classes ended yesterday at Blessed Sacrament, and both Natalie and her mom are happy that she finished sixth grade with mostly Bs, plus an A in Art—and a C in Math! I'd be in trouble if I got even one C, but it's better than Natalie's D– average in Math at SBAMS.

Who knows? Maybe my tutoring actually helped her a little.

Saturday, June 20

Katie and Mackenzie were together at the Hadley Museum for the fireworks.

Dad is down in Washington, D.C., researching some story for the paper. So even though Sam and I are supposed to be at his house, we went to the Hadley with Mom and the Hidalgos. Blanca was a little sad. Her mom is leaving for Argentina tomorrow. But she's not <u>too</u> sad, because in six weeks she'll get to see her mom with me!

Ever since Sam and I were babies, we've gone to the Hadley with Blanca and her family almost every June. The Hadley always has its celebration before things get seriously red-white-and-blue for the Fourth of July. And it puts on the best fireworks ever—not the loud, razzle-dazzle in-your-face-and-all-over-the-sky kind but intricate and quiet and I-can't-believe-it spectacular. And every year Mom and Mr. Hidalgo make the best picnic.

The Larkins usually go to the Hadley with us, too. But this year they went with the Swansons. Katie and Mackenzie came to sit with us just before the fireworks started. I hadn't seen Katie since school ended. She looks taller, or thinner—or both. It was weird. Katie and Mackenzie were dressed exactly alike: white Roxy T-shirts and white denim shorts from the Gap, with identical red Guess? sweatshirts, white ankle socks, and brand-new white Rocket Dog shoes dotted all over with ladybugs. I know those clothes cost a fortune. Since when are Katie and Mackenzie so chummy that they dress like twins? Is that why Katie almost never calls Blanca or me anymore? And the reason she never calls Blanca or me back when one of us calls her?

Mrs. Larkin still doesn't look very pregnant, even though the baby is due in just three months.

Sunday, June 21

I'm so lucky to have Natalie Winter for a neighbor and for my second-best friend.

My Father's Day piano recital was <u>almost</u> a disaster, until Natalie saved me. I don't know if Dad was truly surprised, but he acted shocked that we were having such a big celebration. The Hidalgos came, and so did Natalie and her mom, plus Mrs. Dudley and, of course, Mrs. Howard. Eliot showed up, too. And—surprise!—Katie came with her parents.

The brunch part was great. We ate out back and it was a perfect morning, not too hot or humid. Lots of Mom's flowers are in bloom, and she made featherbed eggs and scones. Mom <u>loves</u> cooking for bunches of people, and I ate way too much. When she cleared the dishes and asked everybody to find a seat indoors, I thought I'd barf for sure.

Everybody squeezed into the living room, and Mrs. Howard set up my music and stood by the piano to introduce me. When she said I would play two of the pieces I've been studying, every bit of music flew right out of my head. My fingers and wrists froze above the keys. I couldn't even remember where to find middle C! Right when I started to tell everybody to come back another day, Natalie stood up, walked to the piano, and said quietly, "For her first selection, my friend Fiona Claire Jardin will play Diabelli's 'Pleasures of Youth.' It's a composition for four hands, and today I am honored to perform the piece with Fiona."

I couldn't believe it! It was almost like Natalie was speaking Swahili. <u>I was so scared.</u> Natalie and I had practiced that piece only twice. But as soon as she sat down next to me and played the first chord, my fingers unfroze and started flying. I've <u>never</u> played like that. When we finished, Natalie stood and said, "For her next selections, Fiona will play Debussy's 'Clair de Lune' and Mozart's Sonata in C Major." Then she squeezed my hand and floated away.

I didn't have to say a word, and I did just what Natalie said I would. Even though I love Debussy and Mozart, I couldn't play those two pieces worth beans. But nobody seemed to care, including me. When I was done playing, I had to stand up and give a little bow. Everybody applauded, and Eliot was the loudest of all.

Sam spelled out a good message on Mom's fridge tonight: FIONA SHINES!

Wednesday, June 24

I got a letter from Miss Dupré.

The letter is way too sad. I don't feel like writing or even thinking about it, so I'm taping it here in my journal:

> *My dear Fiona Claire Jardin,*
> *I've thought of you so often these past few months, and I'm sorry I haven't kept in touch. My father was*

much, much sicker than I'd realized when I left Wilmington in April, and I was quickly caught up in the whirlwind of trying to care for him while learning to say good-bye.

Daddy died on Wednesday morning, the tenth of June. The good news is that he died peacefully. In fact, I'd just let him whomp me at Scrabble, when he said he was feeling tired and closed his eyes to take a nap. My brothers, Leon and Elwood; Miss Olivia (Daddy's sweetheart!); his scruffy old mutt, King; and I were all at his bedside when he passed on. Daddy died with a smile on his face—maybe because he knew he was surrounded by love or maybe because he'd just gotten a triple word-score for spelling zloty, which is some kind of Polish money. My daddy was an outrageous Scrabble player—possibly one of the best in all of New Orleans!

The very day after Daddy died, Tyson, my favorite FedEx deliveryman, brought me the magical book you and Eliot and Joseph and Blanca and all of my angels at Susan B. Anthony Middle School created. Fio, you cannot know how much those poems and stories and wise essays mean to me, especially now while I am struggling to pull myself out of this dark swamp of sadness. I will remember all of you each time I taste a rainbow—and I will savor Taste Rainbows forever, just as I will always treasure our remarkable friendship.

101

I have twenty-six more thank-yous to write tonight,
Fiona—and so I had best bid you adieu for now.

All my love, until rainbows sing,

Jasmine Evangeline Teresa Jefferson Dupré

P.S. Ms. Melissa Smoot enclosed a kind card and
everyone's address with the book. How lucky you are
to have had her for your teacher!
P.P.S. Chloë LaRue Allen and her parents came to a
party my brothers and I gave to celebrate Daddy. She
is so grateful to have you for a friend, Fio. And just
like me, she is eager for you to come visit!

Saturday, June 27

Softball season ended today—thank goodness.

That doesn't sound like great sportsmanship, but playing for the Rockets was way too hard. We won only three games the whole season, and one of those was a forfeit. Dad says that playing for a losing team can build character. Building character isn't half as fun as winning. I feel bad because I knew from the first day of practice that even though we had a few good players, the Rockets weren't strong as a team. Gracie or Twanda or some other Rocket almost always missed or dropped the ball whenever anybody got a hit off me.

The managers and coaches announced the all-stars at the closing ceremonies, and I made the team! I thanked all of them for choosing me, but they'll have to pick another pitcher because I'll be in Argentina in August, during the tournament.

I'm lucky to be chosen as an all-star, but I won't miss the duddy Rockets.

Sunday, June 28

What's going on?

Michael stopped by to show Mom some blueprints and ended up staying for supper. Sam is spending the night at Matt's, and I was so hot and tired, I went to bed early. I flopped around for a long time, imagining how a Popsicle must feel—all sleek and smooth and icy. Pretty soon I <u>wanted</u> a Popsicle, and when I got up to get one Michael was still here.

He and Mom weren't working at all. The lights in the living room were turned down low, and some dorky Gershwin song was playing softly. Mom and Michael were standing by the picture window, and Michael had his arms around her. I made a lot of noise clomping to the kitchen, and when they heard me they started acting all nervous. I asked Mom what they were doing, and she said, "Ummm, dancing?" Then she turned red and asked Michael, "What <u>are</u> we doing?" And he said, "Uhhh, dancing?"

If Mom and Michael were just dancing, why were they acting so strange? And if they were supposed to be working, why were they dancing, anyway?

Monday, June 29

It's definitely <u>not</u> Lucy—or any other friend of Sam's—who's been leaving presents in the milk box.

This morning Mom brought in a piece of pretty paper that had been rolled up and tied with a pink ribbon. It's the Shakespeare sonnet that Miss Dupré made us memorize back in April, the really romantic one that begins:

> *Shall I compare thee to a summer's day?*
> *Thou art more lovely and more temperate:*
> *Rough winds do shake the darling buds of May,*
> *And summer's lease hath all too short a date...*

I forget the rest, but it's about how the poet's True Love is even better than summer because her beauty and goodness are forever. (Besides, she probably doesn't have mosquitoes and stinkbugs, like summer does.) Nobody knows for sure who inspired Shakespeare to write all those romantic poems. Maybe he was sort of like the Secret Admirer, sending mysterious signals to his sweetheart.

It's impossible to tell who left the sonnet in the milk box, because it was printed out from a computer. I thought that Michael had for sure left it for Mom—especially because they were acting so lovey-dovey last night. But Mom said Michael likes some other dead poet named Rumi way better than Shakespeare. (Sam thought Mom said that Rumi was a <u>surfing</u> poet, which sounded cool to him. He lost interest when Mom explained that Rumi lived hundreds of years ago and he was a Sufi, which means he was a mystical Muslim guy.)

Mom also said that sonnet was obviously not for Sam, so I must be the one who has a sweetheart. I doubt it, but the poem did remind me of my valentine. It's been months since I got that shiny gold star, and I still don't know who it's from. The mysterious valentine-giver and the Secret Admirer both like Shakespeare, so he could be just one person—and maybe that person really is somebody who likes me. What if Mom is right? What if I am the one who has a sweetheart? Eliot likes Shakespeare, but I don't know—we spend so much time running together, he has plenty of chances to say something if he likes me. He probably just enjoys having somebody to gab with when he runs.

Whoever the Secret Admirer is, I wish he wasn't so secret.

Thursday, July 24th

Sam and Dad and I leave on vacation tomorrow—and Mom is having a cow.

Sam left Mom a funny magnetic message on her fridge yesterday morning: REMBER SAM AND FIO! (Remember is a pretty big word for Sam to spell. Or maybe he was just being sloppy.) She stopped by Dad's twice tonight to help us pack, and she's called about six times.

Mom brought over a small suitcase loaded with bandages and medicines and nutritious snacks for us to take to Martha's Vineyard. It looks like she cleared out the whole drugstore: calamine lotion, Tylenol, ibuprofen, Kaopectate, Pepto-Bismol, Mercuro-chrome, Ben-Gay ointment, Neosporin, Campho-Phenique, tooth-paste and dental floss, Solarcaine and aloe vera lotion, Q-tips, toenail clippers, tweezers, Band-Aids, and cotton balls. Mom must think we're going on the safari with Mrs. Dudley instead of vacationing on Cape Cod with Dad.

Blanca is stopping by in a while so we can trade pinkie rings before I go. We always swap rings when either of us takes off on a trip. That way we both have a little piece of each other when we're apart. Dad and Sam and I have to get up at five o'clock to-morrow morning so Dad's friend Paul can drive us to Philadel-phia to catch our flight to Boston.

I've packed everything I can think of, but I know I'm forget-ting something important.

Wednesday, July 15

The important thing I forgot to pack for Martha's Vineyard was this journal!

It's been 13 whole days since I last wrote in these pages, and it felt strange not to have my journal with me. I can't remember everything we did, but Dad and Sam and I stayed up late playing Monopoly and Battleship and gin rummy. And we slept in as long as we wanted to—except on our last day, when we had a picnic breakfast (leftover pizza and bouncy Hostess Sno Balls!) at the beach to watch the sunrise. We sailed and fished and hiked and swam and dug for clams. We ate corn on the cob and bluefish and s'mores and strawberry shortcake. We painted with watercolors and built sand castles and told ghost stories and hunted for snipe and went on scavenger hunts with other kids who were staying at Gay Head, too.

Dad only lost his temper once the whole time we were away—the day Sam and I freed the lobsters. Did Dad really believe we could _eat_ Eduardo (Sam's lobster) and Zazu (mine) and Hawthorne (Dad's) after playing with them all afternoon? Dad is big on literary names for everything—especially New England-ish literary names. That's why Sam's rats are Emerson and Melville, and why Dad called his crustacean Hawthorne, for some old dead American writer named Nathaniel Hawthorne.

I could have started another journal while I was away, or I could have written on loose sheets of paper, but I didn't want to. Dad said that maybe it wasn't an accident I forgot to take my journal to Gay Head. Sometimes it's good just to carry memories around in your head and your heart. We brought Mom a Gay Head cap (from Sam), two oven mitts that look like fierce sharks (from Dad), and a little bucket of pretty shells and stones (from me).

It was a perfect vacation, or _almost_ perfect. If only Mom had been with us, too.

Thursday, July 16

Mackenzie Swanson called to invite me to spend three days at her family's new summerhouse on the Jersey Shore.

Duh! Mackenzie Swanson should get a clue. I'd forgotten how pushy she is. When I told Mackenzie I couldn't go to the beach with her, she asked <u>why not</u>. I couldn't think fast enough to figure out a polite reason, so I told her the truth: First I reminded her she'd waved my underwear around in front of my friends, lost my science notes, told <u>everybody</u> I liked Simon, and made fun of Blanca and me. After that I told Mackenzie I don't trust her and I don't consider her a friend. Then I told her to have fun at the beach, said good-bye, and hung up the phone fast!

Dad was right there in the kitchen, having lunch with me, while I was talking. He said, "Ouch!" when I banged down the phone, but then he smiled and hugged me.

Dad doesn't think Mackenzie will be calling back anytime soon.

Friday, July 17

The interesting thing about Natalie is that she's way different from my other friends.

She doesn't care one bit about what everybody else wears or does or thinks. She and her mom like to go to thrift shops and flea markets and antique sales. And even though their house is smaller than Mom's, it's pretty and cozy and happy and filled with music and flowers and paintings and other cool things. Natalie and her mom love Japanese stuff. Natalie has an aunt and uncle who live in Tokyo, and she's spending two weeks with them next month, around the time I'll be in Argentina with Blanca.

Natalie is traveling halfway around the world all by herself, and unlike me she isn't one bit scared to go. Natalie's dad moved to Santa Fe, New Mexico, when she was just six. She's only seen him three or four times since then—and she hasn't seen him at all in the past two years. I can't imagine that. Even though I used to feel sad because Sam and I don't get to see both Mom and Dad all the time, at least we see one of them every single day—and we always talk to the other one every day, too.

Natalie said she was so scared when her dad first left, she never ever wanted to be more than a few feet away from her mom. But after a while she realized that her dad wasn't coming back—and she couldn't spend the rest of her life being scared of everything and everybody. That was around the time when she gave her first piano recital. Her teacher was so amazed by how well Natalie played, she told Mrs. Winter that Natalie should probably study with some famous music professor at the University of Pennsylvania, up in Philadelphia. And she's been serious about playing the piano—and studying music with Mr. Edwards—ever since.

Sometimes I wish I was more like Natalie and less like me. She reminds me of Emily Dickinson because she doesn't give a pickle what other people think. Natalie hardly ever looks at magazines or watches TV, so she doesn't know what's cool. She loves movies, though—old and new. Her all-time favorite is The Princess Bride.

Sunday, July 19

Eliot stopped by this morning to go for a run.

He came back to Mom's house for breakfast, and I showed him the pictures from Martha's Vineyard. Eliot and his parents and two sisters—Eliot is right in the middle, between Charlotte and Emma—are going to Kiawah Island, off the coast of South Carolina, for two weeks in August. His mom and dad are nuts about golf, and Eliot likes to play, too. He said that when you go to Kiawah Island, you mostly sweat and sleep and scratch bug bites and watch the shrimp boats come and go. And when you play golf there, you have to watch out for alligators.

I like miniature golf better. Even though Sam usually smacks me with his ball, playing miniature golf isn't half as dangerous as dodging alligators!

Tuesday, July 21

Just 15 more days until Blanca and I go to Argentina.

I CAN'T DO THIS! I already got all of the shots, have saved $175, and bought a bunch of stuff for the trip, but I can't go to Argentina with Blanca for two-and-a-half weeks. My stomach hurts when I think about those high mountains and trying to stay warm and speaking Spanish and eating strange food and sleeping on mats with Blanca and her cousins. My stomach hurts worse when I think about being 6,000 miles from home. Even though Blanca is my best friend and Mrs. Hidalgo is really nice, there is no way that I, Fiona Claire Jardin, can go to Argentina in two weeks.

What if Mom and Dad get mad because I'm scared? How will I pay them back all that money? And how will I ever make Blanca understand why I can't go? We've been dreaming about going to Argentina together for years.

Wednesday, July 22

It's not the end of the world that I'm not going to Argentina with Blanca—at least I hope that it isn't.

Thank goodness Mom and Dad bought travel insurance, so all the money they spent on my ticket isn't wasted. At first Mom was surprised I didn't want to go, but then she said she should have realized that I was nervous. When I asked her if she and Dad are mad at me because I'm afraid, Mom cried. Then she burst out laughing and shook her head no. She said it's strange how things get so tangled up—that by giving me the one thing they thought I wanted most of all, she and Dad had made me feel scared and sad instead of loved.

Mom says that sometimes it's better to admit you're scared than to pretend you're brave. Worrying all by yourself usually makes trouble seem worse than it really is.

Thursday, July 23

My best friend hates me.

Blanca Lucia Galvez Hidalgo will probably never speak to me again. Mom talked to Mr. Hidalgo last night and told him we'd realized that I'm not ready to take such a big trip. (I'm glad Mom said we, even though I'm the one who chickened out.) I guess Mr. Hidalgo understood why I might be scared, and he said he'd tell Mrs. Hidalgo the whole story when they talk by phone this weekend. Mr. Hidalgo is also arranging to fly with Blanca to Chicago, so she won't have to travel alone to meet her aunt and cousin.

I wanted to write Blanca a long letter, or call her on the phone, to explain the situation. But mom said no way—she insisted that I had to talk to Blanca IN PERSON. So today Mom and I took her out to lunch at Elizabeth's, which is Blanca's favorite restaurant. The pizza was great, like always, and everything was fine—until dessert. That's when Mom said, "Fiona, I know you have something important to discuss with Blanca in private, so I'm going to run a quick errand next door. I'll be back in twenty minutes." I can't believe that my own mother would bail on me like that.

As soon as Mom left, Blanca started talking about Argentina and all the great things we were going to see and do there. She was talking so fast—half in English and half in Spanish—that I could barely understand her. Every time I tried to say something, she talked faster and faster. I think Blanca knew what I was going to say, and she probably didn't want to give me a chance to say I'd changed my mind. But finally I said it, anyway. I told Blanca that even though half of me wants to go to Argentina more than anything, the other half is way too scared.

Blanca didn't seem to hear anything I said after that—about how it's still hard for me to be away from my mom and dad, because I already spend half of the time missing one or the other of them because we don't all live together anymore. And I worry that I'd miss Sam most of all. He's the only person in the whole world who's with me almost every day. I told Blanca I'm scared to go to another country 6,000 miles from home, and I'm scared I might not remember how to say, "Can you help me, please?"

in Spanish. (I'm pretty sure you say, "¿Puede ayudarme por favor?")

When I was done, Blanca was as quiet as a rock. Next she turned pink and her face puffed up like a balloon. Then she started to cry. I've never seen Blanca cry so hard. She told me we're supposed to be best friends, and going to Argentina has always been our dream. Blanca has talked so much about me that her grandparents and all of her aunts and uncles and cousins and everybody else in the village really want to meet me. She said she's spent the past two years worrying about me: Worrying because I was so sad about my parents splitting up. Worrying because we had to move out of our house on Orchard Lane. Worrying because I was afraid Mom and Dad would run out of money, or one of them would move away.

Blanca said that going to Argentina is our big chance to stop worrying and to share our first great adventure since we discovered Babaloneya—or it <u>was</u> our big chance, until I botched everything up. It turns out that Blanca is sick of worrying about me and waiting for me. She said that if I didn't want to go to Argentina with her, I should have said so in June. Then she could have invited Katie instead. <u>Katie and Blanca in Argentina?</u> It's hard to imagine Katie going anyplace that doesn't have bathrooms that lock and mirrors everywhere, so she can check how she looks.

I guess I shouldn't have asked Blanca if she'd forgotten the Code of Babaloneya, because she said <u>I</u> was the one who didn't give a hoot about Truth, Honor & Friendship—No Matter What!

Blanca cried so hard, she soaked three napkins. I told her that sometimes it's better to admit you're scared than to pretend that you're brave. Blanca must have known that was a totally M-O-M thing to say. She replied that sometimes it's better to <u>be</u> a best friend than to <u>pretend</u> to be one. She also said that sometimes friends do things they don't really want to do, just to make each other happy. Blanca <u>hates</u> softball. The only reason she plays is because she knows I love it, and because it's a way for us to spend more time together. Blanca feels the same way about soccer. She likes tennis and swimming way better than softball <u>or</u> soccer, and I never knew it!

Is Blanca Lucia Galvez Hidalgo hiding other secrets from me? And what's a girl supposed to do when her best friend since forever hates her guts?

Saturday, July 25

Even though we're supposed to be with Dad all day, Sam and I had breakfast at Mom's—for Sam's birthday.

Dad is stopping by at noon to take Sam and me up to Philadelphia. We're going to see the Phillies play the Yankees tonight, and Sam's friends Matt and Caleb are coming, too.

Michael had breakfast with us. Sam was grumpy about that, until Mom brought out a platter of French toast with powdered sugar and sprinkles—and eight candles, including one for good luck. Sam <u>loves</u> French toast. And he <u>loves</u> the skateboard Mom got him. (I bet he's getting knee pads and wrist guards from

Dad.) He even likes the model biplane from me. But Sam likes Michael's gift best of all. Even though it looks like just another yo-yo, it's actually a Cheerio Glitter Spin, a famous yo-yo they stopped making a long time ago. The yo-yo is red and it's got four rhinestones, so it <u>does</u> glitter when it spins and sleeps.

That yo-yo was Michael's when he was a kid. Michael was an only child, and he did <u>everything</u> with his parents. His mom got really sick the summer he turned nine, so he spent a lot of time with her in the hospital. His dad gave him a yo-yo for his birthday that summer, and while Mrs. Stevens slept in her hospital bed, Michael practiced yo-yo tricks. Pretty soon he was yo-yoing all the time, and he got really good at it. He even gave little shows for sick kids at the hospital where his mom was a patient, too. Michael ended up with lots of yo-yos, but the Cheerio Glitter Spin was his <u>favorite.</u>

Sam asked Michael if he'd show him some tricks, but Michael looked sad and said that he hasn't touched a yo-yo in 35 years. Sam also asked him what happened when his mom got better. Michael's mom never did get better.

Tuesday, July 28

Mom is mad at me—so what else is new?

Mary-Megan called to ask me to spend the night, but I told her I already had plans. Would it have been better for me to say, "Sorry, Mary-Megan, I can't spend the night because you're boring and I don't want to see your geode collection again"? It's wrong to lie, but I didn't want to hurt Mary-Megan's feelings. Besides, Mom is always saying it's important to be honest—and I honestly can't imagine spending the night with Mary-Megan. She tries way too hard to be funny, and she's so nervous and jittery, she makes me nervous, too.

Does a kid have to be friends with every single person who wants to be friends with her??? Mom thinks I'm being mean and selfish, just because I don't want to spend the night with Mary-Megan. She said that sooner or later I'd be the one who feels left out, lonely, or hurt. Sometimes Mom doesn't have a clue. How does she think it felt to be the sixth-grade woodchuck? How does she think it feels to have Blanca hate me? Mom is the one who lectured me about the difference between friends and acquaintances. Mary-Megan Throckmorton is a perfectly nice acquaintance of mine.

I've already got more than enough friends to figure out.

Thursday, July 30

I've hardly seen Katie all summer.

I wonder how her almost-baby sister or brother is doing. I called Katie three times tonight, but nobody answered. She has her own private line and she's got call waiting. So she must have been on the phone with somebody else when I called. Blanca's phone was busy all night. Blanca and Katie are probably on the phone with each other this very minute, talking about what a loser I am.

I haven't heard from Blanca in a whole week, even though I've called and left messages for her every single day. I also wrote her a long letter and apologized 1,000 times for disappointing her. When we're at Y camp she acts like I'm not even there.

For as long as I can remember, Blanca has been the first and last person I talk to almost every day, besides Sam and Mom, or Dad. Not talking to her is like not eating or sleeping.

Sam taped a HAZMATS poster to his door and a sign that says KEEP OUT. Maybe he should put the poster up in the kitchen instead. Some of his potions are definitely hazardous materials. The one he made this morning was disgusting—chocolate milk with peanut butter, shredded coconut, and raisins. I don't know why I let Sam talk me into being his guinea pig. He won't even tell me what his dumb potions are for. He just says they're magic, and he wears his pointy wizard's hat and a black cape when he mixes stuff together.

"Abracandelabra and sarsaparilla antimacassar" my foot. (Dad has taught Sam lots of magical chants.) Sam's potions don't taste like magic. They taste like garbage. If Sam was a real magician, he'd turn Blanca Lucia Galvez Hidalgo back into my best friend.

Tuesday, August 4

Blanca doesn't hate me!

The doorbell rang after dinner, but when I opened the front door, there was nobody there. Right when I was about to close the door, I saw something purple and white and yellow at the top of the steps. It was a bunch of daisies and pansies in a big jar,

117

with a purple ribbon around it. I went to pick up the flowers, and that's when I heard the glider creaking on the porch—and when I saw Blanca moving back and forth!

I sat down on the glider with her, holding the flowers in one hand and Blanca's hand in the other. And then I started to cry. I told Blanca 100 more times that I'm sorry I turned our dream into a nightmare. She cried buckets, too. And she said she's sorry she's been so mad and mean, but she couldn't help it. At first she was furious, then she felt sorry for herself, then she was sad and lonely and confused, just like me.

Blanca said that I don't know what it's like to worry about being chubby and to have everybody—including me—expect you to be bubbly all the time. She also said I have no idea how hard it is for her to have to explain stuff to her dad lots of times, because he still speaks Spanish way better than English. Even though Blanca is my best friend, I had no idea she worries about those things. As soon as she started to talk, I could feel my heart getting lighter, like it was tied to a balloon and happy to be floating.

Before Blanca left I gave her one of the two bracelets I've been beading all week. Blanca and I—a.k.a. Pansy and Daisy Spit!—have been best friends since we were babies, and she says we'll be best friends until we're grumpy old grannies in rocking chairs. Blanca leaves for Argentina in the morning for more than two whole weeks. I'll miss her so much. But now that I know we're friends again—and now that we've traded pinkie rings and have matching bracelets—it's a little bit easier to let her go.

Thursday, August 6

Katie finally spent the night, and now I wonder why I wanted her to sleep over at all—she's a big crab.

Her mom dropped her off before dinner last night. Mrs. Larkin is all chirpy about the baby. It's due in just five weeks. Katie said her mom has gained 17 pounds. She made it sound like gaining 17 pounds is disgusting. But Mom told Katie that's not much weight to gain when you're pregnant. Mom put on 21 pounds with me and 24 pounds with Sam. Granny Jardin gained 32 pounds with Uncle Harvey! Besides, Mrs. Larkin barely looks pregnant. She's still as tiny as a munchkin. And Katie is skinnier than ever. She's REALLY skinny—so skinny she looks like she might fall over or blow away. When I asked if she'd gotten taller or lost weight this summer, Katie just shrugged and said she hasn't lost as much weight as her mom has gained, like it's a contest.

We had barbecued chicken, scalloped potatoes, sugar snap peas, and salad for dinner, but Katie hardly ate a bite. She cut everything up into little pieces and then pushed the food around. And she asked for her salad on a separate plate, with no dressing. (Katie doesn't like juice from one food slopping into juice from something else.) She wouldn't even touch Mom's peach cobbler.

Mom told us to go chase fireflies with Sam while she cleaned up. We caught dozens of lightning bugs, then let them all go. Later, when Mom tucked us in, she hugged Katie and said it was like the old days in Babaloneya to hear her laughing in the backyard. After I turned out the light, Katie didn't say a word. I thought she'd already fallen asleep. But a few minutes later, she whispered my name. Then she asked if I ever pray. I do pray, especially at church, but she meant do I pray when I need help or if I'm in trouble. When I said sure, Katie asked me to pray really hard, every day, for the baby to be a boy. (If it's a boy his name will be Benjamin. If it's a girl she'll be Victoria.) I told Katie that I'm not too sure about praying for a boy baby—either a boy or a girl will be good.

I think she wanted to change the subject, because then she asked me if I ever dream about french fries or lasagna or hot-fudge sundaes. That's so weird. I never dream about food. I dream about penguins and dancing sunflowers and swimming at the lake. Sometimes I dream I'm pitching or kicking a soccer ball or running with Eliot. I dream about singing with Dad, or chasing Gully and throwing Frisbees with Mom and Sam. And sometimes I dream about all four of us—Mom and Dad and Sam and me—sitting on the front porch of our old house on Orchard Lane, waiting for our lost dog, Snippers, to come home.

Katie didn't seem too interested in my dreams. She got up out of bed and turned on the light. She stared at herself every which way in the mirror, then she asked me if she looks fat. Fat? Get real! Even though she's as skinny as a stick, Katie said she's on a secret diet and she wants to lose 11 more pounds. Katie made me double-dog promise I won't say a word about her diet. She made me swear and cross my heart and spit over my shoulder.

What if the Larkins' baby turns out to be Victoria instead of Benjamin? Why doesn't Katie want a sister? I've always wanted a sister more than anything, even though I'd never trade Sam for one. Mom would know what to do about Katie and her secret diet, but Katie made me double-dog promise not to tell <u>anybody.</u>

Why is Katie acting so strange? She sort of scares me.

Friday, August 7

Sometimes too much information is <u>too much.</u>

Mom always says that Sam and I are lucky because Dad is a good journalist and he's taught us how to dig for facts. But I don't feel too lucky right now. While Dad was tucking Sam in, I flipped through Dad's medical encyclopedia and found out way more than I want to know about an eating disorder called anorexia nervosa. It's most common in adolescent girls, and you can die from it. Sometimes a girl starts out wanting to lose just a few pounds, but after a while she decides to lose more and more weight. So she eats less and less food, and she exercises a lot.

Some girls with anorexia chop up their food and mess around with it. And some talk about food all the time and even dream about it. Some make themselves throw up after they eat. Without even realizing it, a girl can start starving herself. At least Katie doesn't memorize the nutrition labels on cans and boxes, or make lists and lists of the food she eats so she can keep track of every single calorie. Besides, Katie is too young to be an adolescent. Aren't adolescents about 15 or 16? Or am I thinking of <u>juvenile delinquents?</u>

Maybe Katie is so concerned about her weight because she thinks that if she's skinny she'd skate better. But there's no way Katie can lose 11 more pounds—she's too skinny already.

Saturday, August 8

Sam and Dad and I had a nice surprise at the farmers market.

We were searching for the best peaches when I heard somebody say, "Fiona Claire Jardin?" And it was John Robert! I hadn't seen him in almost a year. He helped me to believe that things could actually turn out OK when I was so scared because Mom and Dad were getting divorced.

John Robert looks just the same, except he's a little chubbier and he has more gray hair. He had his daughter with him. Her name is Sally, and she must be about Sam's age. She looks just like John Robert, but with curly hair and no mustache. She wears glasses, like John Robert does. And her eyebrows go up and down when she talks, like his do. When John Robert introduced us, Sally said, "So, are you in therapy?"

John Robert took Sally aside to talk to her in private. When they came back, Sally said, "Excuse me for asking such a personal question. That was terribly inappropriate." She sounds very grown-up, but she sure acts like a six- or seven-year-old. She and Sam made faces at each other while John Robert talked with Dad and me for a few more minutes.

I wanted to ask John Robert if he knows what to do about a

skinny girl who hardly eats anything. But if I'd asked John Robert that, Dad would have made me tell him who I'm worrying about. So instead I asked John Robert if maybe I could call him sometime. He said sure. I should definitely phone John Robert. He'd know just what to do about Katie. But I can't call him. Once I start talking I'll tell John Robert everything.

I promised Katie I wouldn't say a word—and True Friends keep their promises no matter what.

Monday, August 10

Why does the Secret Admirer leave stuff only on Mondays?

Probably because whoever leaves the junk must know that Monday is the only day anybody looks in the milk box—it's the only day Mr. Busby delivers to Mom's house. Maybe Mr. Busby is the Secret Admirer—ha! If so, he's the crabbiest secret admirer ever—and the crabbiest milkperson in the United States of America.

Today there was a bar of lavender soap and a tiny card that had L-A-U-R-E-L written inside a pink heart. That means the presents from the Secret Admirer have definitely been for M-O-M! I said that Dad might be the Secret Admirer, but Mom thinks that's silly—and Sam agrees, because Dad is way too busy doing the tango with Liza to be leaving presents in the milk box for Mom. I don't know who the Secret Admirer is, but these goofy surprises are getting annoying.

I got a postcard from Eliot today. It had a cartoon of a big alligator chomping on the words KIAWAH ISLAND, SOUTH CAROLINA. I've never been to Kiawah Island, but Eliot says it's got mosquitoes the size of hummingbirds, and alligators as big as old Chevrolets. Eliot is always very poetic.

Blanca is in Argentina. Eliot is in South Carolina. Natalie leaves for Japan tomorrow. And Katie is no fun. What am I going to do for the next two weeks? If I'd known that I wasn't actually going to Argentina with Blanca, I'd be playing softball with the all-stars this week. But I'd better not complain to Mom and Dad about not playing. And I'd better not grumble that Mom arranged for Mrs. Dudley to hang out with me on Monday mornings for the next few weeks. Sam stayed home from Y camp for the day, just so he could see her. Mrs. D. has been back from Africa for a week, but she must think she's still there. She showed up this morning in clompy boots and a safari outfit—including a strange helmet with mosquito netting hanging from it!

Even if Mrs. Dudley is a little odd, Sam and I were glad to see her. She learned how to trumpet like an elephant in heat!

Friday, August 14

Maggie had her birthday party at the swim club.

It was so fun! Mrs. O'Neill didn't even hang around. She paid extra for the two cool lifeguards, Austin and Chris, to watch out for us. And there was hardly anybody else at the pool all afternoon. So we got to blast the music over the loudspeakers, and we ate pizza and cake around the pool. Plus Maggie's mom said we could charge any extra food we wanted. Anne Marie, Dawn, Stephanie, Maggie, and I all had chocolate shakes and fries and onion rings. Katie ordered a no-fat peach smoothie, which she didn't even drink. And she didn't get into the pool at all. Even though it was 98° out, she stayed all covered up in a long-sleeved shirt and baggy jeans—all white, of course—and a big floppy hat. Katie always used to get the best tan in the summer. But she said everybody knows that being in the sun causes cancer, so she doesn't take any chances by exposing her skin anymore.

Katie Larkin definitely doesn't take any chances by having F-U-N. I don't know why she even bothered to go to Maggie's party. Her mom probably made her go. Katie barely looked up from her book the whole time, and she was mad that her mom came into the pool area to pick her up instead of meeting her out front, like they'd planned. Now Mrs. Larkin looks pregnant for sure! She's chubby all over and a little wobbly when she walks, like a duck. I told Katie her mom looks cute. I also told her she's lucky because soon she'll have her very own brand-new baby.

Katie made her famous sourpuss face and told me to get real.

Sunday, August 16

Granny called Mom this morning.

I tried to tell her that Mom was out walking Gully, but Granny kept talking and talking and calling me Laurel. I said it was me, Fiona—not Mom—but Granny jabbered on about some hooligans

125

taking Uncle Will's wagon. She said, "Those Clancy boys next door are mean and naughty hooligans, and they could use a good spanking to make them fly right!"

Granny lives on the tenth floor of her apartment building. I don't know why she'd have a wagon up there. Besides, Uncle Will is 40-something, so why would Granny still have his wagon? And there aren't any kids where Granny Ryan lives—just grannies, mostly, who have glasses and fluffy hair, like she does!

I told Mom that Granny had called, but I didn't tell her about our strange talk. Mom worries that Granny is getting too old to live alone. And Mom has been so busy because she and Michael are remodeling their offices, she hasn't been driving up to Philadelphia to see Granny or to bring her down here to visit as much as usual. Uncle Will and Aunt Lily live near Granny Ryan, so they see her all the time. Whenever Mom says she's worried about Granny, Uncle Will says Mom is imagining things. He says that Granny is as good as pie. But Granny doesn't seem as good as pie. She seems more like fruitcake, sweet but nutty.

One more week until Blanca and Natalie come home!

Monday, August 17

There was another present from the Secret Admirer in the milk box this morning.

It's a pretty silver hair clip, a long oval with flowery curlicues and tiny pearls at each end. It looks old, like maybe it belonged to somebody's granny. Mom called Sam and me into the kitchen to tell us the clasp is beautiful. She said she's loved every surprise and we're the best kids ever, but the hair clip looks expensive and we should return it. Then Mom hugged Sam and me. We tried to tell her we don't know one thing about the clip, or about any of the other surprises—and we don't!

Mom put the clasp back into its Milk Duds box and left the box on the kitchen table. Michael swears he hasn't been leaving surprises for Mom. If Michael Edward Stevens isn't Laurel Rose Ryan's Secret Admirer, who is?

Wednesday, August 19

I got a letter from Chloë LaRue Allen.

Her parents' divorce is final, and she and her little sister, Madeline, are moving from their grandparents' house into their dad's new home. It's a small guest house behind a fancy mansion near Tulane University. (That's where Miss Dupré's father used to teach!) Chloë is nervous because she's not too sure when she and Madeline will get to see their mom. Mrs. Allen travels a lot with her band, so the judge who was in charge of the divorce decided that Chloë and Madeline should live with their dad for now.

I tried to write to tell Chloë that even though things might seem bad, maybe everything will all turn out OK. But no matter what I wrote, it sounded lame. So instead I painted a funny picture to cheer her up. (Penguins wearing sunglasses and body-surfing should make just about anybody laugh.) It's Chloë's birthday in three weeks—she'll be 14!—so I sent her a blank journal, too, with three big daisies pressed inside.

Soccer practice starts tomorrow. I'm playing for the Falcons, and Dad is going to help Coach Davies. She's about the only girl who can boss Dad around. That's because she knows everything about soccer, so Dad has to listen!

I wish Blanca loved soccer like I do, but she didn't sign up to play this season. She's going to swim for a team at the Y instead.

Monday, August 24

Blanca got home late last night and came over for lunch today—and Natalie gets home tomorrow!

Blanca had a great time in Argentina, especially during the four days she helped round up cattle on her uncle's ranch. Even so, it sounds like she missed me as much as I missed her. She French-braided my hair, and I tried to do hers, too. But the more I braided, the rattier her hair looked. It was so hot—over 100°!—that Blanca and I spent the whole afternoon swinging in the hammock out back.

We pretended she was Nefertiti and I was Cleopatra, and we fanned each other and ate frozen grapes and tried to stay cool gliding down the Nile, even though Egypt was hotter than blazes. It was too hot to talk or even to think. But when a breeze stirred the air a little, Blanca said she'd stopped by Katie's house this morning. According to Blanca, even though the new nursery is really cute, with sweet little lambs everywhere, Katie isn't too excited that baby Benjamin or Victoria will be born in a few weeks.

It makes me nervous even to think of Katie. I didn't say a word about her, but Blanca watched me for a minute and it was like she knew what I was thinking, anyway. She said, "Friends don't gossip about other friends. Right, Cleopatra?" I wanted to tell Blanca about Katie and her secret diet, and that she's really unhappy about the baby. I wanted to say that I hardly ever see Katie anymore, and when I do she seems mad or grumpy or sort of far away. But I just said, "Right, Nefertiti. Friends <u>do not</u> gossip."

Mom and Sam are out in the garden, picking beans and tomatoes and squash. I'm here in the living room, at the rolltop desk. I'd forgotten about these papers tied up with ribbons—the True Friend lists Mom made us write on New Year's Day. My list and Sam's are pitiful. Mom's list didn't make sense to me in January, but now it's like she was writing a message about Katie and me.

Mom wrote that a True Friend:

1. <u>Sees</u> you with her heart.
2. <u>Listens</u> to you with her heart.
3. <u>Knows and loves</u> you with her heart.
4. <u>Carries</u> you in her heart.
5. <u>Opens</u> her heart to you.

My heart feels heavy and sad when I think about Katie. And now it's thumping and thudding so fast, because just thinking about Katherine Leigh Larkin scares me—like one of us is lost.

Sunday, August 30

It's a total gyp that school starts tomorrow—it's not even Labor Day yet.

I opened the present Miss Dupré gave me before she left. It's the coolest snow globe, from New Orleans, to go with my collection. It's actually a glitter globe, which makes sense because it doesn't snow in New Orleans. Miss Dupré also wrote me a card back in April: *"Fiona, wish you were here. Please come visit soon. Until then, have a great year, O most awesome seventh grader! With love and a hug, Jasmine Evangeline Teresa Jefferson Dupré."* I can't imagine a Language Arts teacher who's even half as cool as Miss Dupré, but I hope the new one knows more about good books and grammar—and about almost-teenagers—than Ms. Smoot does.

Mom isn't wild about today's refrigerator message from Sam: SCHOOL STINKS! She's trying to help him think up a more positive message, but he doesn't like her suggestion: BRAIN POWER!

Monday, August 31

Mr. Riley Riddle, the new Language Arts teacher, is TOTALLY cool!

I have Mr. Riddle the very first thing every day, for Homeroom/Advisory and for Language Arts—just like last year with Miss Dupré and Ms. Smoot. This is what he'd written on the blackboard: HOW IS A LANGUAGE ARTS TEACHER LIKE A JUDGE?

Blanca and Katie and Anne Marie and Maggie and Eliot and Dylan and Luke and Joseph and a bunch of other kids I know have Mr. Riddle for Advisory and for first period, too. When

Mackenzie Swanson tried to sit next to me, I told her that desk was saved for Blanca. Mackenzie made a prissy face. Then she said she'd dumped Simon over the summer, like I care, and went to sit next to Katie.

We spent half of Language Arts talking about what _we_ want to do in class this year. Then Mr. Riddle told us things _he_ wants to do—like helping us to figure out how short stories work and how to write movie reviews and song lyrics. This year, for Mr. Riddle, we have to write in our journals for at least 15 minutes four days a week, and spelling counts.

Joseph Tucker is so rude! He asked Mr. Riddle if <u>Riley Riddle</u> is his real name. Mr. Riddle said that for as long as he can remember, people have teased him about his name—like it's a bad joke. (Mr. Riddle's official name is Riley Montgomery Rawlings Riddle III. Why do so many Language Arts teachers at SBAMS have such long, strange names???) He also said that sometimes people assume things about other people because of their names or how they look or dress or where they live. When Mr. Riddle was 11 or 12 and lots of kids made fun of his name, he decided to make his name a <u>good</u> kind of joke. That's when he turned himself into the Riddle Man. He has hundreds of riddles to make us think about how interesting, fun, and tricky the English language can be. For example: "<u>Question:</u> How is middle school like the queen of England? <u>Answer:</u> They both have subjects!"

Mr. Riddle is going to write a riddle on the blackboard every day. He has a plastic armadillo on his desk, with a hole in its back and a little sign: FEED ME! At the end of class, anybody who guesses the daily riddle can write down the answer, sign the slip of paper, and put it in the armadillo. If you're right you get four bonus points—and when you have 20 points, you win a free pass from doing a grammar work sheet.

When the bell rang at the end of the period, Mr. Riddle asked if anybody had figured out today's riddle. Eliot was the only one who got it: Language Arts teachers and judges both assign sentences!

Friday, September 4

Seventh grade is way too hard!

Even though it's a holiday weekend and it's only the first week of school, I have a ton of homework. My schedule is like last year's but different, too:

7:30–8:00	Homeroom/Advisory (Mr. Riddle)
8:05–9:00	Language Arts (Mr. Riddle)
9:05–10:00	Math (Ms. Willis)
10:05–11:00	Spanish (Señorita Diaz)
11:05–12:00	P.E. (Coach Henry)
12:00–12:30	Lunch
12:35–1:30	History (Mr. Andrews)
1:35–2:30	Science (Ms. Wright)

All of my teachers seem nice and interesting, but teachers almost always seem good the first week of school. Ms. Willis is trying to convince us that math is like poetry. She said her goal this year is to inspire kids who think they don't like math to get excited about it. Ms. Willis said, "I hope all of you will learn to appreciate the logic and beauty of math." The logic and beauty of math?

Who cares about the absolute value of −16? What's so beautiful about 16, except that's how old I'll be when I get to drive in three years and 270 days—but who's counting?!

Monday, September 7

It's Mom's favorite holiday.

Not really, but she always makes Sam and me clean out our closets, dressers, and desks on Labor Day. Sometimes I wonder who made up these holidays, anyway. We haven't been in school long enough to need a break yet. If kids were in charge of things, we'd get an extra day off for Halloween each year, just when the days start to get short and gloomy—and when school begins to seem like too much work.

We had an all-day soccer clinic on Saturday, to get ready for this week's season opener. It's a good thing I've been running for the past eight months, because Coach Davies and Dad made us do a lot of tough drills. Most of the other girls couldn't keep up, but I did OK—and I wasn't one bit sore afterward. Dad thinks the Falcons are going to be a great team. I just hope we play soccer better than the Rockets played softball.

I was worried that soccer wouldn't be much fun without Blanca, but there's a new girl named Lola Jeffers who's playing for the Falcons—and she's awesome! She's in three of my classes, too: Math, P.E., and Science. When I told Mom that Blanca isn't playing soccer this fall but a new girl named Lola is, she said, "One chapter ends and, as the page turns, a new chapter begins—all in the same book of your life!" Mom has been spending way too much time around Michael Stevens.

I called Katie to see if she wanted to go bike riding with Mom and Sam and me this afternoon, but Mrs. Larkin said Katie had spent the night at Mackenzie Swanson's and wasn't home yet. What is the deal with Katie and Mackenzie?

Thursday, September 10

I saved Lola Jeffers a place at lunch.

Lunch is annoying sometimes, because everybody makes a big deal about sitting together. It must be hard for a new kid to know where to sit. Blanca, Anne Marie, Maggie, and I almost always sit on one bench, with Dylan, Joseph, Luke, and Jamil on the other side of the table. Sometimes Eliot eats with us, too, and some days Katie—except now Katie Larkin hardly ever goes anywhere or does anything without her new best friend, Mackenzie Swanson.

Lola seems a little quiet and shy. When I first heard her talk, I thought she was for sure from New Orleans, like Miss Dupré. But Lola laughed and said no, she's from Brooklyn, in New York City! Her granny lives in Louisiana, though, and her mom grew up there, so at least it wasn't a totally feeble question.

Lola is a good name:

Lola Monique Jardin

VICTORIA IRIS LARKIN WAS BORN AT 10:07 THIS MORNING!

Mom picked me up at school and we got to see Victoria in the hospital. <u>She is so little and so cute.</u> She has tiny ears and toes and fingers and everything else. She weighs just 6 pounds, 14 ounces. And she's $16\frac{5}{8}$ inches tall, or long. Victoria has lots and lots of hair. It's thick and black and spiky, not one bit like Katie's long blond hair. Victoria looks like a punk rocker, and she can screech like one, too.

Katie didn't say a word the whole time Mom and I were at the hospital. She wouldn't look at Victoria, or her mom and dad, or her grandma and aunt. And she refused to hold Victoria, even though she's her very own baby sister. Katie looked mad when I tried to rock Victoria a little—until Victoria cried so loud that I gave her back to Mrs. Larkin. Mom took a picture of the three of us, but I bet it's a stinker, because Victoria was bawling, Katie was grouchy, and I was nervous. Mr. Larkin was handing out cigars to everybody. He was in a big rush because he had to get back to the courthouse. (Mr. Larkin is a lawyer and he's in the middle of a big trial.) Katie's grandma and aunt wanted to stay with Mrs. Larkin and Victoria, so Katie came home with Mom and me.

After dinner Katie and I went to my room to do homework. She started brushing her hair and looking at herself in the mirror, as usual. Then Katie asked whether I'd been praying for a boy, like she'd said to when she spent the night a few weeks ago. I told her I'd forgotten about praying for Benjamin. Besides,

Victoria Iris seems like a great baby. Katie said, "Some friend you turned out to be, Fiona!"

Victoria Iris Larkin is definitely a girl—and that definitely was NOT part of Katie's plan. What is Katie going to do?

Saturday, September 19

Dad and Sam and I stopped by Katie's house after my soccer game.

Dad hadn't met Victoria until today. He bought her a sleeper that looks like a tiny Phillies uniform. He also got her a genuine Phillies cap, even though Victoria won't grow into it for about 12 years. Dad bought Katie a present, too, a University of Pennsylvania sweatshirt. Mr. Larkin went to law school at Penn and he wants Katie to go there, so she can be a lawyer, like him. But Katie has already decided to go to Pratt Institute, in Brooklyn. She wants to study fashion design and photography, so she can be a professional fashion photographer someday. Katie has had a plan for her life since she was six years old, but I guess Mr. Larkin has a different plan for her.

Vicky—that's what Mr. and Mrs. Larkin call her—was cranky, so we didn't get to see her do much. Katie calls her baby sister Yicky Viris, instead of Vicky Iris, when her mom and dad can't hear! She says Victoria is a big pain, because she cries and pees and poops all the time, and she can't do any tricks.

On the way home from the Larkins', Dad asked me what Katie

has been up to. He misses her at soccer games, and I guess he misses her just hanging around with me, like she used to do. Dad smiled and said he still remembers all the fun that Katie and Blanca and I had during our summer in Babaloneya. I wanted to ask Dad if he thinks Katie looks too skinny. I wanted to ask what can happen if a girl goes on a secret diet. And I wanted to ask if a really smart and mostly normal girl can maybe have anorexia. But I just said I don't see Katie too much anymore, because I'm busy with soccer and she's busy with skating and Victoria and whatever.

We won today, 8–7, against the Vipers. Lola scored three goals and I scored two. My second goal went right in from a corner kick, and it put us ahead with just two-and-a-half minutes left in the game! Dad was right—the Falcons are great!

Monday, September 21

Katie and Mackenzie hate each other's guts!

I'm not too sure what happened, but Blanca is going to call me right after Anne Marie calls her, once she's talked to Maggie, who's supposed to be talking to Katie this very minute. I'm pretty sure Mackenzie saved a seat on the bus for Dylan, and that's what started the ruckus. Anyway, Dylan sat next to Mackenzie, instead of sitting next to Katie like he usually does on the way home.

Mackenzie has been hanging around near Dylan's locker after school. She jokes around with Katie a lot and tries to get Katie to dress like her, but everybody thinks Mackenzie—a.k.a. the Black Widow (the code name Blanca and I made up for her)—is more interested in Dylan Gregory Matthews than in Katherine Leigh Larkin. I could have told Katie that Mackenzie is BAD NEWS, but it wouldn't have done any good. Katie wouldn't believe me—about Mackenzie or about anything else.

Tomorrow is Mom's birthday. She'll be 38. Sam and I got her a bottle of her favorite perfume—with a little help and a few dollars from D-A-D! I need to finish the card.

Thursday, September 24

KATIE IS IN SERIOUS TROUBLE!

I went over to the Larkins' after school because Mrs. Dudley has the flu and couldn't take Sam and me to Dad's. I shouldn't have done it. I should never have looked at Katie's journal. I wasn't trying to snoop. Honest. But there was nothing else to do. Mrs. Larkin needed Katie to help with Victoria, so I had to wait alone in Katie's bedroom for about 20 minutes. Her journal was open on her desk, and I accidentally flipped through a few pages.

The only entries in Katie's journal are lists and lists of foods with numbers next to them. All of the entries are kind of the same, like this:

Breakfast

1 poached egg	75
¾ cup of cornflakes	75
½ cup of skim milk	44
tea	0

<u>Lunch</u>

10 grapes, peeled	25
2 slices of turkey on 1 slice	
of wheat bread	180
1½ cups of popcorn	100
water	0

<u>Snack</u>

apple	80
diet soda	1

<u>Dinner</u>

broiled chicken breast, no skin	120
iceberg lettuce, no dressing	25
½ cup of steamed rice	120
1 cup of skim milk	<u>88</u>
	933 CALORIES

300 sit-ups
Ran 6 miles/46 minutes
50 minutes/exercise bike

Katie had written a total, like 882 CALORIES or 1,047 CALO-RIES, at the end of each entry. Every day with more than 1,000 calories had a big red **X** through it. And every single page had notes about hundreds of sit-ups and jumping jacks, or miles of running and bike riding.

1,000 calories? No healthy kid can live on 1,000 calories a day. (Coach Henry says that most 12-year-old girls who are growing need about 2,200 calories a day, or more—especially if they're active and athletic.) Katie always complains about being fat, even though she's as skinny as a noodle. She talks about food all the time, and she messes around with it and dreams about it, but she hardly ever _eats_ any. I promised I wouldn't say anything about Katie's secret diet. I crossed my heart and everything.

Why don't Katie's mom and dad notice how skinny she is? Why doesn't somebody do something to help her? <u>Why can't anybody except me see that Katie Larkin has anorexia nervosa?</u>

Friday, September 25

Today was a total disaster.

We had to get timed on running the mile in P.E., so we can compare today's time to how fast we run at the end of the year. Katie finished first, of course—way ahead of everybody else. Mackenzie is really fast, too, and she followed Katie into the locker room. Lola and I finished just after Mackenzie.

Katie and Mackenzie HATE each other more than ever. I guess that while Katie was showering, Mackenzie hid her clothes. By the time I'd finished showering, there were a bunch of girls in the locker room, and they were all watching Katie and Mackenzie squabble. Katie was wrapped in a wet towel and shivering all over. She was yelling at Mackenzie to give her clothes back. When Katie called Mackenzie a fat pig, Mackenzie dropped Katie's clothes in a heap on the floor, pushed her, and yanked her towel away. <u>Katie was standing there totally naked.</u>

Everybody started screaming, especially Katie. She looks like a shrunken old skeleton. Every single bone and rib sticks out, and it's almost like you can see through her pale gray skin. Mackenzie yelled for somebody to go get Coach Henry from the track. And all the other girls were shrieking and screaming, "Oh my god!" and "Look at Katie!"

Katie ran back into the shower stall, and I could hear her sobbing. I grabbed her towel and tossed it over the top. Blanca and Lola gathered up Katie's clothes and handed them to her over the top, too. And Mary-Megan yelled at Mackenzie and all those other girls to mind their own business! She said Katie has been sick, so she's lost a bunch of weight. Then I said Katie is feeling lots better, and she's getting stronger. And Blanca said that if Mackenzie doesn't watch it, she and Mary-Megan and I are going to kick her butt once and for all!

I guess Blanca and Mary-Megan and I must have scared everybody, because nobody said another word. By the time the rest of the girls came in from the track with Coach Henry, Katie was dressed and Mackenzie was out in the hall, waiting for the bell to ring. Katie started walking toward the cafeteria with Blanca and Lola and Mary-Megan and me, like nothing was wrong. But then Katie grabbed Mary-Megan by the arm, and the two of them hurried into the cafeteria by themselves. I didn't see Katie or Mary-Megan for the rest of the day. Maybe Katie told Nurse Burnham she didn't feel well, so she could go home. I hope so.

I was surprised that Mary-Megan would come to Katie's rescue like that. I didn't even know that she and Katie are friends, but it turns out that they've been practicing to start a hip-hop band.

When she's not flipping over math and her geodes, Mary-Megan plays the electric bass!

Blanca is coming over in a little while to spend the night. We've got to figure out what to do about Katie.

Saturday, September 26

I'm not the only one who has been worrying about Katie all these months.

It turns out that Blanca knows all about Katie's secret diet, too. She even saw Katie's weird food journal, and Katie made her double-dog promise not to say anything, either. Blanca and I stayed up really late trying to decide what to do. We figured we could:

1. Tell Mr. and Mrs. Larkin there's something really wrong with Katie.
2. Tell my mom or dad, since they know the Larkins better than Blanca's parents do.
3. Call John Robert for advice.
4. Tell Nurse Burnham that Katie has been starving herself.
5. Not do anything, except cross our fingers and pray for Katie to be OK.

It wasn't until we went out on the balcony and I saw my Jasmine star shining so bright that I knew for sure what to do: call

Miss Dupré in New Orleans. But by that time it was too late, so Blanca and I called her when Dad dropped us off at Mom's this afternoon.

We phoned Miss Dupré collect, like she said I could. Blanca dialed, but I did most of the talking. Miss Dupré's brother Leon answered the phone. He said, "Hey there, Fiona!"—like he knew all about me. Then he said "Jazzy" was running an errand, and she'd be back in an hour. I told him that Blanca and I were actually calling because of an urgent situation. And Blanca asked Leon to please, <u>please</u> have Miss Dupré call us back at my mom's as soon as possible.

Miss Dupré will know what to do. Blanca and I had to call her. Blanca is out back digging for worms with Sam. I'm supposed to be getting ready for my soccer game. <u>I hope Miss Dupré calls back soon.</u>

Sunday, September 27

Katie says I'm a mean, rotten liar.

She called a few minutes ago, right after Mom got home from talking to Mr. and Mrs. Larkin. Katie said she's never ever going to speak to me again—and the same goes for Blanca. But Blanca and I didn't tell on Katie, at least not exactly. When Miss Dupré phoned back yesterday, I just said that Blanca and I have a friend who knows a girl who's really, really skinny. Blanca told her about how our friend found a journal with lists and lists of foods and calories in it—and about how our friend had accidentally seen the skinny girl naked in P.E., and the skinny girl looks sick and awful and scary.

The more Blanca and I talked to Miss Dupré, the more worried I got about Katie. I started to cry so hard that I couldn't even speak. Miss Dupré was quiet for a minute. Then she said, "Fiona and Blanca, is Katie in trouble?" I was too scared to say yes, but Blanca said, "How did you know, Miss Dupré? We didn't tell you—we promised not to say a word!" Miss Dupré said, "Sweetie pies, I've got two eyes, just like everybody else. If I were a betting kind of woman, I'd bet that Katie Larkin has been struggling with some big trouble for a mighty long while. Trying to be perfect is a hard, lonely job." Miss Dupré promised she wouldn't call Katie or her parents, but then she asked to speak to Mom in private.

Mom was on the phone with Miss Dupré for half an hour. But she didn't say anything about Katie or Miss Dupré until after my soccer game late yesterday afternoon. (We won, 7–2, against the Sharks, but who cares?) Mom talked to Dad all alone for a few minutes once the game was over, and then Sam went with him to spend the night. When Mom and I got home, she told me to wait in the garden while she made a pot of tea. For a while we just sipped tea and nibbled on snickerdoodles. Then Mom started asking lots of questions about Katie: When did I first realize that she was unhappy? How long has she been dieting? What does she eat?

I told Mom that I'd promised Katie not to say anything about her secret diet, and then I started to cry. Mom talked very quietly and slowly, like she was thinking about every word. She asked if I truly care about Katie. Of course I do—we've been friends for nine whole years, since we were three. Then Mom asked if I honestly believe I'm helping Katie by keeping her secret. I had to say no. And when Mom asked if Katie can solve her problems all by herself, I said no once more.

Mom was on the phone for a long time last night, talking to Miss Dupré again, to Dad, and to Blanca's mom because she's a doctor. She called Mrs. Larkin this morning and then went over to Katie's house after lunch. Mom was gone all afternoon, and when she got home, her eyes were red and she was snuffly, like she'd been crying. Mom didn't tell me what happened, but she hugged me and said she's proud of Blanca and me for caring so much about Katie and for trying to help her.

Mom says that Katie is lucky to have friends like us. <u>Friends?</u> Katie Larkin hates our guts.

Sunday, October 4

Michael came over for supper.

He and I played cribbage while Mom helped Sam with his book report. One good thing about Michael is that he doesn't make you feel like you have to talk all the time. Sometimes when Michael and I are both being quiet, it's like he can tell what I'm thinking. Tonight I was wondering if Katie is OK, and trying to figure out what I can do so she'll get better and stop hating me. That's what I was thinking when Michael blew me off the cribbage board. And that's when he said some old Buddhist guy once told him that if you sit quietly, not doing a thing, spring will come and the grass will grow, all by itself. I guess that means there's not too much I can do right now to help Katie. Maybe it's up to her to try to get better. And maybe it's up to me to wait patiently while she does.

Michael asked me an odd question, like he does lots of times. He wanted to know whether I'd followed my head or my heart when I decided to talk to Miss Dupré about Katie. My head definitely told me <u>not</u> to break my promise to Katie, so I told Michael I must have been following my heart. He nodded and said, "Precisely, Fio. And if you follow your heart, more often than not it will take you where you're meant to go." When I told Michael that Katie hates Blanca and me, he shook his head no. He said <u>hate</u> is a very powerful four-letter word, just like <u>love</u>—and for most people, both hatred and true love are rare.

I hope Michael is right. I hope Katie doesn't have it in her heart to hate me.

Wednesday, October 7

Blanca just called to tell me Katie has quit ice-skating.

Mary-Megan must be the only person Katie talks to at all anymore. She told Blanca that, for one thing, Katie isn't strong enough to compete now, and for another, she <u>hates</u> ice-skating. I can't imagine Katie not skating. That would be like Blanca quitting Argentina, or Natalie quitting piano, or me quitting soccer—

except it's <u>way</u> worse than me quitting soccer. Katie Larkin is one of the best skaters in the whole state of Delaware. She loves ice-skating more than anything.

At least I always thought she did.

Friday, October 9

Katie came back to school.

She got the weirdest haircut. It's all choppy and lumpy, like she'd hacked her beautiful blond hair off herself. It's strange— now she almost looks like a boy instead of a girl.

Katie's locker is only three away from mine, but we might as well be on different planets. Between Language Arts and Math, she pretended she didn't even see me. She just kept doing the combination on her lock over and over again. She didn't say one word to me all day. I don't think Katie talked to anybody, except Mary-Megan and Nurse Burnham. She floated like a ghost from class to class. And she wasn't in the cafeteria at lunchtime. (Mary-Megan said Katie has to have lunch in the nurse's office. Maybe Nurse Burnham keeps a list of what she eats—and what she doesn't—for Mr. and Mrs. Larkin.)

Sam fell asleep right after dinner, and Dad challenged me to a game of chess. He and Mom <u>both</u> know how to tweak me when I'm stuck in a funk. I asked him if he's ever had a friend who didn't want to be his friend anymore. He said, "Well, Sarah Bailey—except she did call me to have lunch last week, which surprised me. And your mom, I guess. Even though we got divorced, she's the best friend I've ever had—maybe the best friend I ever will have." Mom? It seems like she and Dad are still OK friends, even though mostly they talk about Sam and me.

When Dad had lined up all of his black pawns, he said, "Don't give up on Katie, Fiona. Stick with her. Sometimes you've got to fight with all your might to hang on to what's important to you. And remember, Fio-bean, sometimes friends are like cows: If you want them to come home, you've got to give them plenty of space, so they can graze."

Cows grazing? That sounds like something Michael would say. I didn't tell Dad that, though. And I didn't ask why he and Mom didn't fight with all their might to hang on to each other—instead of fighting so hard to tear each other apart.

Saturday, October 10 ⚽

We lost in overtime, 4–5, to the Sonics.

It was our first defeat of the season, but at least I played well and scored the first goal of the game. Lola scored two goals and had two assists, including the one for my goal! I've already scored five goals this season, and scoring isn't even my main job. I play sweeper, so mostly I steal the ball and move it up the field to Lola and the other forwards. I like playing sweeper, because I get to cover the whole field. And when I'm running, I can feel the wind in my hair—and everything else is a blur. It's easier for me to move fast this season, because I've been running so much and trying to keep up with Eliot! Even though we played our best, it's no surprise the Falcons lost today—the Sonics are <u>super.</u>

Mom and Michael are almost done remodeling their offices. They're having a big party next Saturday to celebrate being partners in their new business.

Sunday, October 11

I ran four whole miles with Eliot!

We finished in a little more than half an hour, and the time went so fast, it seemed like we'd barely run <u>two</u> miles. Eliot knows a lot about running, and he says I'm a natural. (He's training at the high school with the junior varsity cross-country team this year.) I don't know about that, but I guess I <u>am</u> lucky to have long legs, like Dad's. And I'm for sure lucky that because of Eliot's coaching, my arms and legs don't go flying every which way, like Gully's do!

We cooled down by jogging, then walking, around the pond. All the color drained from Eliot's face when he saw that the whole south side of the pond is being dug up. Last week Mom told Sam and me that somebody is building condos there, but I guess Eliot hadn't heard the news. Mom isn't happy about it, and Eliot is even more upset. He's lived by the pond his whole life, and he says it's always been his backyard treasure.

Sam and Mom and I have lived here for only two years, but I know what Eliot means. In the fall the oaks and maples turn bright red and yellow, and the wet earth smells rich and dense. When the pond freezes over in winter, it's almost like our private skating rink. We collect pussy willows and cattails around the pond in the spring, and on summer nights, Sam and I chase tree frogs and listen to whippoorwills along the grassy banks while crickets sing their good-night.

Mom says that having the pond nearby is almost like having a tiny piece of the ocean in your pocket.

Tuesday, October 13

Natalie is the queen bee at Blessed Sacrament!

Her mom had to go to work early this afternoon, so Mom and Mrs. Winter arranged for Mrs. Dudley to pick Natalie up along with Sam and me. Natalie was supposed to be in the BS office at 3:15, but she was late, as usual. Mrs. Dudley and Sam went out to the playground while I waited in the office for Natalie—all alone with Mother Agnes. She's in charge of the whole school. And no offense, but she looks like a big pug with glasses. I was sweating the whole time I was sitting there, with a statue of the Virgin Mary staring at me from one corner and Mother Agnes at her desk in front of me, asking lots of questions.

Mother Agnes must be smart, because after I told her my name, she said, "Ah, Irish and French—now there's a feisty combination!" She asked me what faith I am, and I wasn't too sure what to say, but I told her that all four of my grandparents are

Roman Catholic, which is true, even though Pappy Ryan is dead. She smiled, sort of, and asked what parish my family belongs to.

That's when I really started to sweat. I didn't want to explain that Mom says she feels closer to God in forests and meadows than in church. Or how Dad and Sam and I usually go to a Presbyterian church near Dad's town house because the choir and the music are great and the sermons aren't too long. (Dad calls it the Church of the High Holy Sofa, because the pews are so comfy that he usually naps a little!)

Thank goodness that before I could answer, Natalie showed up with a bunch of BS girls buzzing all around her.

Saturday, October 17

Ryan & Stevens Homescape, Ltd., is <u>awesome!</u>

The offices are really nice, and the grand-opening party was spectacular. Mom and Michael hired a string quartet, and there must have been 200 people at the party. Blanca and I got to help her dad with the catering. We each earned $10. (Plus I got 79¢ as a tip from Dad!) Sam helped the bartender with punch and soft drinks. It was a perfect chance for him to practice mixing potions, even though nobody would try one except Mom and Michael. There were flowers everywhere—including the biggest bouquet of all, to Mom from Dad.

Dad invited Mom to have dinner with us after the party, but she'd already made plans to celebrate with Michael at Toscano.

Dad was surprised (not in a good way) that Mom and Michael named their new business Ryan & Stevens Homescape, Ltd. On the way home he explained that sometimes women keep their maiden names for business and use their married names for everyday stuff. Mom must have forgotten to tell Dad she had her lawyer friend Ann change her name back to Ryan—for business and for everyday stuff, too.

Sam snuck a present into Mom's new office. It's a big picture of him and Dad and me on the front porch of the house we rented at Gay Head. Dad bought a frame for it, and Sam put the photo on Mom's desk, right next to a picture of him and Gully and me. And he put Mom's favorite picture of her and Michael— the two of them paddling down the Brandywine River in a canoe—in one of her desk drawers.

I bet Mom will be surprised when she finds that photo of us on her desk on Monday morning!

Sunday, October 18

I had a feeling it was a bad idea, but Dad wouldn't listen.

He thought it would be fun to surprise Mom with breakfast in bed. He knew she'd be tired from her big party last night. And he figured she'd be happy to see us—him and Sam and me—with fresh orange juice and warm bagels and strong coffee and the New York Times. (Sam was all excited about the idea, too—probably because we got to skip church.) Dad packed everything in a pretty wicker basket, and he bought one red rose on the way to Mom's house, to put in the basket with the newspaper and the food. That seems like something the Secret Admirer would do! Dad figured that Mom would be thrilled when we rang the doorbell and said, "SURPRISE!" I wasn't so sure. Mom always likes to know what the plan is, including for surprises.

Mom was definitely surprised. She was still in her bathrobe when she answered the doorbell, even though it was almost 8:30. She wasn't wearing her ratty old terry-cloth robe, though. She had on a pale purple one, with yellow and pink flowers all over, and it barely covered her up. Mothers are not supposed to wander around half dressed on Sunday mornings. They're supposed to make big breakfasts and then scurry about getting ready for church, except that Mom quit going to church years ago—and Dad still makes a stink about it. Anyway, Mom looked a little foggy, as if she didn't quite know who we were. And her hair was sticking up funny, like a porcupine's quills. But once she realized that it was Sam and Dad and me at the door, she smiled and told us to come in. Dad said we had a surprise for her, and Sam and I hustled into the kitchen to set the little table.

That's when things got weird. We could hear the shower going and somebody singing—a guy singing. Dad suddenly got very quiet. He said that maybe it wasn't a good day for a surprise, and that we—him and Sam and me—could go to Clancy's for breakfast instead. Dad told Mom he'd drop us off at noon, like he usually does. Just then Michael sort of danced into the kitchen. He was dripping wet and had a towel wrapped around his waist. It took him a minute to realize that Sam and Dad and I were in the kitchen with Mom. He said hi to my dad, whistled to Sam, and winked at me. (At least I <u>think</u> he was winking at me. Michael wasn't wearing his glasses and his eyes were squinty, so it was hard to tell who he was looking at.) Then he backed out of the kitchen, real quiet, and Gully followed him.

Mom started scuttling around and jabbering about making chili and watching the Eagles game. I knew something was fishy, because Mom would rather clean the oven than watch the Eagles play the Jets. Sam asked why Michael was taking a shower at our house. Dad coughed a fake cough and said he'd forgotten that Michael was going to help Mom clear out the garden. He said, "Right, Laurel?" But Mom didn't answer. She just held up the thermos and said, "Coffee?" Mom doesn't believe in little white lies—or any other kind.

Mom walked Sam and me out to Dad's car. Dad told her that the next time we have a surprise, we'll call ahead to make sure it's OK. Even though he apologized about six times for the confusion, he didn't sound sorry. He sounded sad—and mad. <u>Dad does not like Michael Stevens at all.</u>

I called Natalie a bunch of times this afternoon. First her line was busy, and now no one is home. Today is Natalie's birthday, and she and her mom are coming over for supper. Natalie is the first one of my good friends to turn 13! Where is she? Maybe Mrs. Winter and Natalie are already on their way.

I hope so—I can't wait for a big piece of the apple-spice birthday cake Mom and Sam and I made!

Tuesday, October 20

While we were doing the dishes tonight, Mom asked if I wanted to talk about her and Michael.

The answer is N-O! I told her that Sam and Dad and I had made a deal—Dad agreed to keep Liza or Marcy or whoever he dates separate from Sam and me. Mom said that sounds like a good plan. But then she said she doesn't think that she and Michael are actually dating. If they're not dating, what are they doing? Even though they work together, they also ride bikes and go to movies, they eat dinner together—and half the time they drag Sam and me along with them. Does Mom think I don't know where she is when I call her house late at night and nobody answers?

I like Michael OK. He's nice and smart and thoughtful, and sometimes he's funny. But Michael Stevens is not part of this family, even if Mom spends the night with him sometimes when Sam and I are at Dad's.

Saturday, October 24

We ended up at Michael's house for dinner again.

Nobody said anything about him showering at Mom's house a week ago. I thought Sam would for sure say something rude, but he just asked Mom if she'd heard from the Secret Admirer lately! Mom told Sam he's silly and changed the subject—to dinner. She loves cooking in Michael's kitchen. It's big and sunny, and the stove and everything else is shiny and new. She said she'd make chicken cacciatore if everybody stayed out of her way so she could cook and listen to opera. Sam and I always stay out of Mom's way when she listens to opera, because she usually sings along. Sorry, but Mom is just about the worst singer I've ever heard.

Michael showed Sam and me all of his fishing stuff while Mom cooked. One whole end of his barn is full of rods and reels and spinners and waders and other fishing gear. Michael knows everything about fly-fishing. He ties his own flies, and he explained how he uses tweezers and special magnifying glasses to tie really delicate ones.

Sam asked Michael if cutting the guts out of fish is gross. But Michael has never gutted a fish. He doesn't keep or eat the fish he catches—he releases them right back into the water. Michael said that more than anything he likes to imagine being a fish. Sam thinks that's totally stupid, but I think I know what Michael means. It must be cool and gentle to live in a clean stream or a river or a lake—with sunlight shimmering down and the current carrying you along to someplace you've never been before. Grass and weeds bow and wave as you glide by. And every once in a while, a fly or some other bug catches your eye. And you're so hungry, you dart to the surface and bite. What a bummer to chomp on a yummy-looking fly or a worm and then end up with a hook in your mouth instead.

Michael says that, for him, fishing has nothing to do with catching fish. He likes the waiting, and the quiet that settles around him and inside of him as he imagines a sleek fish in clean water. That's how running makes me feel—calm and quiet and empty and light. And sometimes writing in my journal makes me feel like that, too. Sam did <u>not</u> want to listen to Michael and me talk about fishing and running. He asked Michael to show him how to tie a grasshopper fly, but Michael said that tying a fly takes a lot of patience.

Sam decided to play with his Game Boy instead.

Sunday, October 25

Eliot called this morning to see if I wanted to go for a run after lunch.

We didn't go until three o'clock, and it was after four when we got home. Mom asked Eliot to stay for supper! At first I was mad—it seemed like another one of Mom's dumb ideas. But he said sure, and we all actually had fun. Eliot and I helped Sam with his homework while Mom made dinner. We had mulligatawny and apple crisp, and the whole house smelled like curry and cinnamon and apples baking.

We helped Mom do the dishes, and then Eliot and I waited out front, on the glider, for his dad to pick him up. It was a beautiful autumn night, clear and brisk, with the leaves on the trees rustling and the stars sparkling. Eliot played his harmonica, and I told him about my Jasmine star. He wanted to know which star it was, so I pointed it out—at least I <u>think</u> I showed him the right one. It's hard to tell for sure without Dad's telescope.

Eliot went home more than two hours ago, and my heart is still thumping. What made it so happy? The starry night, the cheery music, Eliot—or all of those things?

Monday, October 26

I'm going to start getting up at dawn on Mondays so I can catch Mom's dweeby secret admirer.

This morning there was a small package with a pink stone heart inside. It's a pretty little heart, with a nice message on the tiny card: FOR LAUREL—FROM MY HEART TO YOURS. But now Mom almost seems irritated instead of surprised when she finds anything except butter and yogurt and cottage cheese in the milk box. She thanked me for the stone heart, but I told her again that I don't know anything about any of the gifts. Then she hugged Sam, but he shrugged and asked Mom to pass the milk for his shredded wheat.

Mom put the heart on the windowsill. It shimmers in the sunlight, all shiny and smooth.

Thursday, October 29

This is NOT good—I have serious B.O.

Recently I've smelled something stinky everywhere I go, and I suddenly realized that maybe I stink. So I paid Sam $1 to smell my armpit. He sniffed around for a minute, and then he said, "P.U.! Your pit smells like Emerson's and Melville's cages when they're dirty." Great. I smell like a dirty rat's nest. That's plenty of

158

bad news for one day, but Sam also mentioned that I've grown two bumps on my chest! At first I thought my sweatshirt was just lumpy, but those two bumps are definitely M-E. I for sure didn't have bumps when I went to bed last night. How did this happen?

Just two more days to Halloween, so we get to dress up for Language Arts tomorrow. Mr. Riddle says he'll give us extra credit if we come to class as somebody—a writer or a character—from literature. I can't decide whether to be Emily Dickinson, or Miss Havisham from Great Expectations. Either way, I can wear this old gauzy white dress of Mom's with a lacy white shawl, and lots of powder to make me look frail and sort of ghostlike.

Mom thinks I'm too old to go trick-or-treating, but I don't!

Wednesday, November 4

What's the point of math?

Adding and subtracting are OK, even regular multiplying and dividing. But who cares about inverse operations and dividing by fractions and working with percentages? Here's the so-called tantalizing extra-credit problem Ms. Willis gave us for homework: "Franklin is making quiche for dinner. He has 2 pounds of ham and $1\frac{1}{2}$ pounds of cheddar cheese. How many quiches can he make if the recipe for one quiche calls for $\frac{2}{3}$ of a pound of ham and $\frac{1}{2}$ pound of cheese? Will Franklin have any ham or cheese left over?" That dumb problem is about as tantalizing as pork rinds.

Mom says it's important for every kid to know math backward and forward. Mary-Megan's mom is an accountant. She knows everything about math, and so does Mary-Megan. Why don't people just hire an accountant when they need help with money or math? If I could hire Mary-Megan to do my math homework, I'd have more time to play the piano, practice doing headers, and teach Gully new tricks. I'd rather write poetry than divide numbers to ten places. Besides, Franklin's recipe is gross. Vegetarians like me won't touch quiche with ham in it. Who cares if Franklin has ham or cheese left over?

There are way more important questions about this silly problem: Who is Franklin cooking for? Is he using egg whites only? And what's for dessert?

Monday, November 9

I saw Katie going home with Mary-Megan and Mrs. Throckmorton after school.

Katie and Mary-Megan were both laughing, and Katie looked almost happy, until she saw me. Mary-Megan waved, but Katie looked the other way. I bet they were on their way to Mary-Megan's to play music. Two girls are not a band. I'm a good singer and I can really rock on Dad's electric keyboard. But who wants to be in their goofy band, anyway?

At first I felt scared for Katie, and then I felt sad. But now I'm mad at her, too. Mad that she's been so mean to Blanca and me. Mad that she's been so selfish and doesn't care at all about her friends or anybody else. Mad that she could be so hateful about sweet little Victoria. Mad that somebody so smart could be so dumb. And mad that she would do something that could really hurt her forever.

Just thinking about Katie makes me want to shake her and hug her at the very same second. But I'll <u>never</u> get another chance to hug her. So instead I'm here all alone in the dark, writing under the covers with a flashlight.

Thursday, November 12

It looks like Sarah Bailey is back in Dad's life.

Her Martha Stewart apron is on the peg in the kitchen, and Dad's freezer is loaded with her yucky casseroles—like Sam and I wouldn't notice? Three are labeled TOFU SURPRISE. Two others are TUNA OLÉ. <u>They all stink!</u> And Sarah bought Dad a bunch of candles, some herbal tea, and aftershave that smells like cloves.

Sam and I have already done the Sarah thing with Dad. Now Sam is busy mixing up some NO SARAH potions. Why would Dad want to get tangled up with her again?

Saturday, November 14

The Falcons won today, 9–6, against the Fireballs—in the last game of the season.

I can't believe we beat the Fireballs. They were undefeated, until today. I scored two more goals. That makes nine goals and 12 assists for me in ten games this season! Coach Davies wants to enter us in a tournament over Thanksgiving, but almost everybody—including me—is going away for at least part of the holiday weekend. She wants the Falcons to play in the spring league, too, and she's going to try to work with us once a week all winter.

I love soccer and I really like playing for Coach Davies, especially with Lola on the team. But I don't want to think about next spring. If I play soccer then, I can't play softball. Mom thinks it's good for me to play two sports I love. But Dad thinks it's time for me to choose, so I can get <u>really</u> good at soccer or softball instead of being <u>pretty good</u> at both. Everybody seems to have an opinion about what I should do with my life. Next spring I'll be almost 13. Next spring I, <u>Fiona Claire Jardin,</u> will decide whether to play softball, soccer, both, or neither.

Maybe I'll learn to play tennis with Blanca!

Monday, November 16

The teachers had a staff development day, so we didn't have school.

Mom took the day off, too. I can't remember the last time we spent a whole day together without doing errands or chasing Sam and Gully around. After we dropped Sam off at his school, Mom and I came home and made scones and tea. It was pretty out, cold but clear, so we had breakfast in the garden. Then we took Gully for a long walk and climbed over the piles of dirt at the south end of the pond.

Mom is gloomy about the condos. She said that maybe it's a good thing we've been renting our house. For a while she was thinking about buying it, but not anymore. We've only lived here for two years, <u>but I don't want to move again.</u> Even though

Mom's house is only half as big as our old house on Orchard Lane, I like it. Everything is comfy and cozy. Besides, Natalie and her mom are our neighbors—and Eliot lives close by, too.

But maybe if we did move, at least the Secret Admirer wouldn't know where to find us! Mom brought in a little silver bell from the milk box this morning. It's a Christmas tree ornament, and it was wrapped in paper covered with holly. Mom put the bell on the windowsill in the kitchen, next to the bath salts, the lavender soap, the hair clip, and the stone heart. (She ate the chocolate, and I don't know what she did with Shakespeare's mushy sonnet.) Doesn't the Secret Admirer have a calendar? We're still eating Halloween candy, and it's not even Thanksgiving yet. Who has time to think about Christmas?

Maybe Mom's secret admirer is Santa Claus. Ho-ho-ho!

Thursday, November 19

HOW IS SUSAN B. ANTHONY MIDDLE SCHOOL LIKE A LOAN FROM THE BANK?

That's what Mr. Riddle had written on the blackboard before class this morning. We spent most of Language Arts diagramming sentences, like this one:

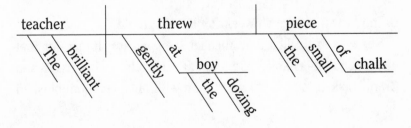

I like to diagram sentences. It's so tidy to pick out the subject, the predicate, and the direct object (if there is one). Everything else—the adjectives and adverbs and prepositional phrases—is just extra stuff. Mr. Riddle is always talking about the simplicity and grace of a carefully crafted sentence. And Ms. Willis is still yammering about the logic and beauty of math. The two of them should get together, so that grace and beauty could rule forever!

I tried to think of an answer to Mr. Riddle's riddle, but nothing made sense. I haven't figured out even one of his riddles. Eliot got today's riddle, like he always does. He told me after class that both Susan B. Anthony Middle School and a loan have prin-cipals. I know Ms. Harris is the principal at school, but I didn't have a clue what a principal has to do with a loan. Dad told me I could figure it out if I used my head and the dictionary. Some-times Dad is a pain! I checked the dictionary, and it sounds like the principal is the lump of money you pay interest on when you borrow money.

Dad should pay Sam interest every time he slides coins out of Sam's piggy bank!

Sunday, November 22

Granny Ryan is here all week for Thanksgiving.

She wasn't thrilled that Michael was over for dinner—or that he's spending Thanksgiving up at the cabin with us. When Granny asked Mom what's going on with Michael, Mom blushed and got all fidgety. Mom told Granny that she and Michael have been friends for more than ten years. Granny said she's not talking about friends. She wants to know when all the smoochy stuff began and what Marty—that's what Granny still calls Dad!—thinks about Michael.

Mom started banging the dinner dishes around in the kitchen sink. (We have a dishwasher, but Mom almost always washes the dishes by hand. She says that washing dishes is relaxing, even though she's usually either cranky or daydreaming when she's sloshing around at the sink.) Mom told Granny that she doesn't have any idea what Martin—that's what Mom still calls Dad when she's mad!—thinks about anything, except she knows that he likes the Phillies and the Green Bay Packers, and he loves Sam and me more than anything.

Mom reminded Granny that she and Dad have been divorced for two whole years, and they were separated for six months before that. Then she told Sam and me to go finish our homework, even though neither of us had any to do. I was glad Michael had already gone home, because Granny said something mean about Mom finding one of the only Buddhists in all of Delaware to "be sweet on," and why couldn't she just wake up and work things out with Dad?

Mom said Michael isn't a Buddhist—he's just very interested in Eastern thought and culture. So then Granny asked why, if Michael isn't a Buddhist, he always talks about Buddha-this and Zen-that—and besides, how does Mom know for sure that he's not a Buddhist? Mom thought for a minute, banged a few more pots together, and growled, "If Michael Stevens were a Buddhist, he wouldn't love fly-fishing!" Then Mom asked Granny how can <u>we</u> be sure she's not a Komodo dragon?! Granny stuck out her tongue like a big lizard and went to look for Sam.

It's going to be a <u>long</u> time until Granny Ryan goes home next Sunday.

Tuesday, November 24

Something isn't right with Granny.

She's always been a little absentminded and silly. She loses her keys a lot, and she calls everybody by the wrong name. But now she forgets more important things—like where she is and who she's talking to. She does strange stuff and dresses weird, too. Granny has worn the same clothes since Mom went up to Philadelphia to get her on Sunday: two scarves (yellow and black, like a bumblebee), a purple sweatshirt, and a ratty old green skirt over red sweatpants. Even when she's indoors, Granny wears red rubber boots and the chartreuse hat she used to wear on ski trips.

Mom was crabby at breakfast this morning. When I asked what was wrong, she said she'd been up half the night. She woke up at two A.M. and found Granny on the front porch. Granny was wearing one cow slipper and one rubber boot, and she had an apron on over her nightgown and a parka on top of everything. She told Mom it was time for mass. Then she said that Paddy— that's what Granny always called Pappy Ryan—would be coming any minute to take her to Saint Paul's. But Pappy died more than five years ago. And Saint Paul's is the little church near Granny and Pappy's old house in Philadelphia. That's where Mom used to go to church when she was a kid. Granny hasn't lived in that house or gone to that church since way before I was born.

Mom acted like Granny is mixed up because she's not in her own apartment. I wanted to make Mom feel better, so I said Granny has <u>always</u> been a little mixed up. But Granny is way more confused than ever. When I got home from school, Mom was poking around in her garden—and Granny was in the kitchen, staring at the microwave. I asked Granny what she was doing, and she said, "I'm waiting for <u>Star Trek</u>." Granny wasn't joking. She kept watching the microwave, like Mr. Spock would turn up any minute. Sam said he wanted to watch, too. He loves <u>Star Trek</u>, but I bet he was just trying to make Granny happy by sitting with her.

I didn't tell Mom about Granny and the microwave. Maybe Granny will feel better tomorrow. She's only 71. That's not so old. And even if she is a little nutty sometimes, who cares? Granny Ryan and Mama Jardin are the sweetest, gentlest, best grannies ever.

Miss Dupré called to wish me a happy Thanksgiving, and to ask about Katie. Too bad that Katie still isn't talking to Blanca or to <u>me.</u> Mary-Megan says that at least Katie is doing a little better. And even though it's only been two months since the nightmare with Katie and Mackenzie in the locker room, Katie doesn't look quite so scraggly and scary.

Wednesday, November 25

We—Mom, Sam, Granny, Gully, and I—drove up to the cabin this afternoon.

Gully got carsick, as in barf-barf-barf every 20 minutes. Granny hummed the whole way from Wilmington, <u>really</u> loud and <u>really</u> off-key. She never stopped, not for one minute. Mom turned the radio way up. I guess she was trying to drown out the barfing and the humming and Sam's whirring Game Boy. So for two hours I got to listen to a bunch of people on <u>All Things Considered</u> jabber about Thanksgiving traditions.

Granny's humming, Sam's whirring, Gully's barfing, and NPR jabber. No wonder my head still hurts! Maybe I should have stayed home with Dad. He and Sarah and I could have made a fresh batch of Turkey Olé for Thanksgiving dinner. Blech. But Dad is having Thanksgiving at the shore with Mama and Papa and a bunch of the other Jardins. And <u>I think</u> he gave Sarah the heave-ho. The apron is gone!

Uncle Will, Aunt Lily, and my cousins Emily and Molly met us at the cabin this afternoon. They brought the turkey and almost everything else, except the pies. Mom <u>always</u> makes the pies, and they're always perfect, even though she never measures any of the ingredients.

That's why Dad used to call Mom the Great Cuisini, Kitchen Magician to the Stars!

Thursday, November 26

This could be the strangest Thanksgiving since the pilgrims and Native Americans ate turkey and venison and lots of other weird stuff hundreds of years ago in Plymouth, Massachusetts.

It wasn't bad, just strange. Mom says we'll always remember today as the Flags-of-All-Nations Thanksgiving. Michael drove up this morning with Gladys and Ralph and two of his and Mom's friends. (I bet Michael and Mom are trying to fix up María and Yee, even though those two speak different languages.) The Hidalgos also came up this morning. And Mr. Minnelli, from next door, stopped by at noon, just in time for lunch. The turkey was already in the oven, and he kept saying it smelled tantalizing. So Mom asked him to come for dinner, too. He said he didn't want to be a bother—and besides, his son Ernesto was visiting from Pittsburgh with his wife and their teenage daughters, Gina and Andrea. Of course, Mom invited all of them!

Blanca and her little sister, Francesca, and Sam and I spent the afternoon making place cards. Every time we thought we were done, it turned out that we had to make more. We ran out of construction paper, glitter, and feathers. Gully, Gladys, and Ralph ran around like wild wolves. They dragged sticks and dead fish and other stinky stuff in from the lake. Granny kept asking who let the horses in. She wouldn't come out of the bathroom until Mom asked her to help mash the potatoes. By the time we sat down to eat, there were 20 of us, plus three dogs and Mr. Minnelli's two cats.

Mom must have used every pot and pan in the cabin's tiny kitchen—and most of Mr. Minnelli's cooking stuff, too. Granny wouldn't eat anything except tapioca and cornflakes. Mr. Minnelli built a big fire in the hearth, and now Granny is asleep in her rocker. Mom and Michael have about 100 candles burning. Even with dirty dishes piled all around, the cabin looks pretty in the flickering light. Blanca is spending the night and driving back with us tomorrow. And now it's snowing—just enough to make the whole day feel like magic.

It's an almost perfect Thanksgiving. If only Dad and Mama and Papa Jardin—and Uncle Harvey—were here, too.

Saturday, November 28

Today is Katie's 13th birthday!

I wanted to call her this morning, but Dad said that maybe I should make her a card instead, in case she's still thinking about things. He also said that sometimes the hardest part of being a friend is putting out energy when nothing good comes back to you. And he's right—trying to be nice to Katie is no fun when she ignores me all the time.

Blanca came over for lunch, and we both made outrageous birthday cards. After Dad dropped us off at Mom's, Blanca and I rode bikes all the way to the Larkins'. They usually go up to Cape Cod to spend Thanksgiving with all four of Katie's grandparents, but both of their cars were in the driveway. They probably decided to stay home to have their first big holiday with Victoria.

Blanca and I didn't ring the doorbell. We just left our cards at the front door.

I wonder how Katie celebrated Thanksgiving. I wonder if she ate candied yams with mini-marshmallows. I wonder if she ate turkey with cranberry sauce, and pumpkin pie with whipped cream. I wonder if she ate anything at all. I hope so. I wanted to see little Victoria, but I wanted to see Katie even more.

I wonder how Katherine Leigh Larkin likes being a teenager. I wonder if she'll ever speak to me again.

Saturday, December 5

I saw Mrs. Larkin and Victoria at the library this afternoon.

I tried to hide so that Mrs. Larkin wouldn't notice me, because I figured she was probably mad at me, too—for getting in Katie's business. But as soon as she saw me, Mrs. Larkin came right over and hugged me. Victoria was all bundled up on her back, like a papoose with huge eyes. Mrs. Larkin asked if I could go with them to have a snack at the café across the street. I was nervous about talking to her, but I thought it would be rude to say I didn't want to go. So I called Dad and asked him to pick me up at the café instead of the library.

Mrs. Larkin sat sideways in our booth at the café, with Victoria still perched on her back. She ordered two cups of cocoa, and one brownie, for me. Then she smiled and reached across the table to pat my hand. When Mrs. Larkin asked if I'd heard from Katie, I told her no but that was OK because Katie probably was still really mad at me. Mrs. Larkin nodded and said Katie has been having a hard time. Then she said she and Mr. Larkin and Katie have been talking with John Robert all together twice a week. And Katie sees him by herself twice a week, too.

John Robert! When Katie first heard I was seeing him, because of the divorce, she called John Robert a shrink. And she made fun of me because my parents made me go to a therapist. But after the first few times I talked to John Robert, I didn't care what Katie Larkin said about him—or about me. I wanted to talk to him. I hope that now John Robert can help Katie figure out some things with her parents, like he helped me. I guess that having a baby brother or sister be born when you're almost 13 isn't necessarily the greatest thing.

I could tell that Mrs. Larkin didn't want to discuss Katie too much. But I think she wanted me to know that Katie's problems don't have anything to do with me. Mrs. Larkin explained that on that Sunday my mom stopped by to talk a couple of months ago, she and Mr. Larkin made Katie stand on the bathroom scale. Katie weighed only 78 pounds—almost 20 pounds less than I do—but she said she felt as big as a cow! She told her mom that she wanted to get down to 67 pounds. That's what Katie weighed when she won her first silver medal skating in the regionals. That's what she weighed when she was nine years old! Mrs. Larkin took Katie to the doctor the very next morning. She and Mr. Larkin had their first talk with John Robert the same day. I guess Katie is lucky she didn't have to go to a hospital.

Mrs. Larkin thinks Katie is doing a little better. Even though I was glad to hear that, I got a big lump in my throat and started to cry. I told Mrs. Larkin I'd sworn to keep Katie's secret. I'd crossed my heart and spit over my shoulder and double-dog promised not to say a word. That's when Mrs. Larkin started to cry, too. After a long time, she said Katie is extremely fortunate to have friends like Blanca and me, who love her enough and are brave enough to try to help her.

She also said it's probably hard for Blanca and me to understand it now, but when Katie told us about her secret diet—and when she left her journal lying around where Blanca and I could each read it—it was maybe her way of asking for help. Mrs. Larkin thinks Katie <u>wanted</u> Blanca and me to know she was in danger so that we would tell somebody. At first I thought Mrs. Larkin was wrong. But when she asked if I've ever, in my whole life, heard Katie ask for help, I had to say the answer is N-O.

<u>Katie Larkin never asks for help from anybody.</u>

Sunday, December 6

Sam and Mom and Dad and I had dinner at the Hotel Dupont to plan the Christmas holidays.

Dad met us at Mom's house so we could drive downtown together. Sam made everybody sit in the living room, to try one of his secret potions. It wasn't too bad—cranberry juice, with ginger ale and orange sherbet, and sprinkles on top.

The decorations at the hotel are beautiful, like they are every year, and dinner was delicious. We got everything figured out for when Mama and Papa Jardin and Granny Ryan are here for the holidays—which days Sam and I will be at Dad's, and which days we'll spend with Mom and Granny. We were about to order dessert when Dad told Mom she looks pretty with her hair pulled back. Then he noticed her hair clip, the old-looking silver one from the Secret Admirer! He kept staring at the clip, and he said it was very unusual. The more that Dad talked about Mom's hair clip, the lower Sam slumped in his chair.

Mom took the clasp out of her hair and put it on the table. She told Dad she has a secret admirer who has given her several little gifts, including the barrette. Then she winked at Sam and me. But Dad wasn't winking—he was staring at Sam. He was sure he'd seen that hair clip before. Dad was almost positive it was the clip his friend Renée had lost at his town house months and months ago. Mom asked the waiter to bring our check while Dad went to get our coats.

Too bad we had to skip dessert—I wanted chocolate mousse.

Monday, December 7

Dad came over to Mom's after dinner tonight.

I think he and Mom are trying to figure out whether they should punish Sam. Except for Renée's hair clip, Sam didn't steal any of the Secret Admirer stuff he left for Mom. Besides, he didn't know the clip was Renée's. He thought maybe Mrs. Dudley had left it at Dad's after she got her hair chopped off. Mrs. Dudley helped Sam wrap most of the other stuff because she thought he had a crush on some little girl in his class. She even printed out Shakespeare's sonnet on Dad's computer, even though she did think it was an odd poem for seven-year-olds!

Poor Sam. He's been mixing up secret potions and leaving gifts from the Secret Admirer—and studying The Parent Trap—to try to make Mom and Dad fall in love all over again. Sam thought his potions had actually been working. It's true that Dad sent flowers to Mom for her new office, and he asked her out to dinner to celebrate. But it's also true that the more Mom seems to care for Michael, the more interested Dad seems to be in M-O-M.

After Dad had gone home, Mom tried to tell Sam that even though she and Dad like each other just fine—and even though they're nice to each other most of the time—it's not because they're getting back together. Mom said Dad is interested in her work and in her life, and he's especially interested in everything that connects her to Sam and me. But Sam cried and cried, and he wouldn't listen to anything Mom said—probably because he's heard it all 100 times before. It's not going to happen, but Sam still wants Mom and Dad to get married again, so we'd all be together forever.

Mom was quiet for a few minutes, then she asked Sam if he remembers his very first yo-yo. And he said that of course he remembers that yo-yo. How could he ever forget it? He keeps it in a red velvet box, and he loves it more than anything. Then Mom asked Sam why he doesn't ever play with that yo-yo. Duh. He doesn't play with it because he has newer yo-yos that are better and trickier. But when Mom asked Sam if he wants to get rid of his old yo-yo or trade it in for a different one, he said, "No way!" Even though he doesn't play with his first yo-yo anymore, Sam still loves it best. He likes to know just where it is—and sometimes he takes it out to look at, so he can remember the very first time he pulled a yo-yo on a string.

Mom smiled at Sam and hugged him tight. They were both crying, and I was, too. Before he went to bed, Sam said to Mom, "You're like Dad's first yo-yo, aren't you, Mom?" And Mom laughed and said yes, she is—maybe even Dad's very best yo-yo.

Sam and me? We must be like the string that keeps Mom and Dad connected.

Monday, December 14

I got a present from Chloë today.

There was a card inside the package, and she apologized for not writing in such a long time. The past few months must have been really hard for her and Madeline—selling their house, moving into their dad's little guest house, and missing their mom. But maybe things are starting to improve a little. Chloë's mom found a part-time job teaching music and drama at a high school for the performing arts. She doesn't play in her band anymore, except at clubs in New Orleans. And now Chloë and Madeline spend every Sunday night at her apartment. I guess that's better than nothing.

Chloë promised to write more after the holidays. She thanked me a bunch of times for the blank journal. She's already gotten used to writing in it, and now writing for 20 minutes almost every day has become a habit.

Chloë told me to open her present right away. It's so cute—a penguin key chain!

Friday, December 18

HOW IS CHRISTMAS LIKE A COMPOUND SENTENCE?

I finally figured out one of Mr. Riddle's riddles: Christmas and compound sentences both have clauses! No school until January!!!

Saturday, December 19

Dad and Sam and Mom and I spent all afternoon working at Mom's kitchen table.

We decided to wrap a bunch of our Christmas presents together—and we had to finish making the presents for the Jardins, everybody in Mom's family, and our friends. Mom had bought two dozen plain picture frames. We painted the frames and decorated them with stuff we've collected this year—little shells and stones from Martha's Vineyard, feathers and dried flowers we found at the pond and the cabin, and cut-up postcards from the places Dad visited while he was researching stories all over the United States. Dad and Mom sorted through boxes of photos. Then Sam and I picked the perfect picture to put in each frame: Blanca and me, with our hair in French braids, in the hammock (for Blanca). Natalie and me at my piano recital (for Natalie). Sam and Dad and me chasing lobsters in the kitchen at Gay Head (for Uncle Harvey). And Eliot and me on the glider at Mom's (for Miss Dupré)!

I had only one picture of Katie to put in a frame, and it isn't very good. It's the photo Mom took of Katie and Victoria and me at the hospital the day Victoria was born. Victoria is yowling; my eyebrows are squished together, like I'm worried; and Katie is scowling, like she's mad—and she looks all scrawny and gray. Maybe that picture is so sad and scary-looking because all three of us have red eyes. Mom should either get a better camera or take a photography class.

Glurp. Dad and Mom and I must have drunk a quart of Sam's newest potion. Even though he knows there's no way his secret potions—or anything else—will make Mom and Dad get back together, he still loves to experiment with his so-called magic!

Tuesday, December 22

Mom must be part elephant.

She never forgets one thing. After breakfast she made Sam and me stay at the kitchen table to look at the True Friend lists we made last New Year's Eve. Sam said his list is still perfect, and Mom let him go out back to make a snowman—like she agreed with him about the bubble gum and the farts! My list is pathetic. Last January I wrote that a True Friend:

1. <u>Always</u> says nice things about you, agrees with you 100%, and thinks you look perfect.
2. Never gets mad at or disappointed in you—and never keeps you waiting!
3. Keeps your secrets <u>no matter what.</u>
4. Never gossips or passes notes about you.
5. Is exactly like you.

None of the five things that I wrote then seems important now. Well, maybe number four is OK—friends <u>shouldn't</u> gossip. But sometimes friends <u>do</u> get mad at each other, and they definitely don't have to be exactly alike. If all of my friends were just like me, I'd for sure be bored. And just because somebody disappoints you or disagrees with you or even breaks a promise to you—<u>if</u> she or he has a good reason— it doesn't necessarily mean you can't be friends anymore.

Mom's list is definitely the best, but she's 38 and she <u>does</u> know way more stuff than Sam and me put together. A year ago I thought her list was weird, but now maybe I know what she means about seeing and hearing and knowing your friends with your heart. Was I a good friend or a lousy friend this year? I disappointed Blanca, but at least I told her how I honestly felt— scared!—about going to Argentina last summer. I have <u>not</u> been a good friend to Mary-Megan or to Mackenzie, but like Mom says, everybody has to make choices about friendship. Besides, I'm trying to be a friend to Chloë, even though we've never really met, and I'm also getting to know Lola. And even though Natalie changed schools, we're better friends than ever. I want to be a friend to Katie, too, but I know I can't force her to like me—or to forgive me for breaking my promise to her.

There were lots of times this year when I thought that maybe I'd have a different kind of life if I had a different name. Savannah Jasmine Jardin? Viola Juliet Jardin? Lola Monique Jardin? Sometimes I can't believe how stupid I am. I'll never be any of those girls, and I'll probably never be as smart and talented as Katie, as bubbly as Blanca, or as brave as Natalie, but that's OK.

My mom and dad taught me a long time ago that my name is a combination of Irish (from my mom's family) and French (like my dad's). Fiona Claire Jardin means "Light Clear Garden." When I was ten I felt more like a dark foggy weed patch, but now that I'm almost a teenager—maybe my life is like a garden that's just about to bloom in the sunlight.

Wednesday, December 23

Sam fell asleep halfway through It's a Wonderful Life.

He'd rather watch The Terminator any day, but Dad and I like old-fashioned holiday movies. He and I bundled up to have cocoa and watch the stars from the balcony while Sam slept on the couch. Dad hauled out his telescope so I could check on my Jasmine star—she's as bright and as glorious as ever. And he reminded me how lucky I am to have so many stars and so many friends in my life, even if they're not all close by every second of every day. Dad says there are whole new galaxies of stars and friends, just waiting for me to discover them!

Mom and Dad and everybody else gave me lots of advice about friends this year. But it was Michael who gave me the wisest advice of all when he told me one of his sort-of Buddhist sayings: "In walking, just walk. In sitting, just sit. Above all, don't wobble!" According to Michael, it's impossible to be a True Friend until you know who you are. It feels like I've been wobbling a little all year, but I'm beginning to realize that I'm still absolutely me, Fiona Claire Jardin—and that's who I'll be next year and the year after that and on and on until forever.

I called Miss Dupré to wish her a merry Christmas, but I wonder how <u>merry</u> her holidays can be without her father. Maybe she'll see a bright star in the sky tonight—my Jasmine star!—and she'll feel the love shining down on her. And maybe I'll wish on my star for her to come back to Wilmington to teach at SBAMS next year. If Miss Dupré met Mr. Riddle and they fell in love, she could be Jasmine Evangeline Teresa Jefferson Dupré Riddle. Or he could be Riley Montgomery Rawlings Riddle Dupré.

Or they could both just stay totally who they are and live <u>very</u> happily forever after!

Friday, December 25

I'm beginning to wonder if somebody is going to run away from home every Christmas.

Last year it was Sam. This year it was Granny Ryan, even though Granny didn't actually run away—she wandered off. It was still dark this morning when I heard Sam yelling to tell Mom that Santa had left the front door wide open. When Mom realized that Granny was gone, she pulled on her boots and her big down parka, right over her nightgown. She told me to watch Sam until she got back, and then she scooted out the door. The longer Mom was gone, the more scared I got. After half an hour I turned the TV on to some goofy boys choir singing Christmas carols, and I told Sam to stay put for 15 minutes. I told Gully to stay, too—and I knew Gully wouldn't move until I told him, "Good boy!"

I don't know why, but I headed straight for the pond. When I got to the end of Mom's street, I heard a faint voice. It was Mom calling "Help!" I kept running, faster and faster, all the way around the pond to the big piles of dirt, and there were Mom and Granny, sitting high up on one of the bulldozers. First I made sure they were OK, and then I told them to keep warm and not to worry, because I'd be right back with help. I was too scared to cry—or to stop running.

When I got back to Mom's house, Dad was inside with Sam and Gully. Sam was still sitting on the couch. He was crying and he said he'd only moved once, to call Dad when I hadn't come back after 16 minutes. Gully hadn't budged an inch. I told Dad about Mom and Granny on the bulldozer. He said for Sam and me to wait right there, with Gully, but we followed Dad out to his car. Gully jumped in, too! I didn't realize it until then, but I'd run all the way to the pond and back to Mom's—almost four miles—in just 27 minutes!

When Dad stopped the car, Sam and Gully and I ran straight to Mom and Granny. Dad was right behind us, and he climbed up on that bulldozer to help Granny down. She didn't seem one bit surprised to see him. And she didn't seem to think it was odd or dangerous that she had wandered off in the dark and climbed up on a bulldozer on Christmas morning. Dad wrapped his coat around Granny and then climbed back up to help Mom.

Mom was crying when she hugged Sam and me, but Granny was laughing and happy. She hugged Mom and Dad and said, "Oh, Laurel and Marty! What a beautiful sunrise, what a glorious Christmas morn!" Then she hugged Sam and me, too. And it was beautiful, with pink and purple streaking across the sky as the sun started to poke through the clouds. Sam wanted to know if he could watch the sunrise from up on the bulldozer. In his dreams. Gully barked and licked everybody—even Dad!

One of the mysterious things about Christmas is that it never turns out like you think it might. Everybody was so worried about Granny, nobody said a word about the ring that Michael gave Mom last night—nobody except me. It's a beautiful ring, with sapphires and sparkly diamonds. It's the prettiest ring I've ever seen. Mom said it's an heirloom that belonged to Michael's great-grandmother, then his grandmother, and then his own mother. When I asked what that beautiful ring means and why

Michael gave it to her, Mom took a deep breath and said it means that Michael loves her as much as she loves him.

That's when we both started to cry.

Saturday, December 26

We decided to celebrate Christmas today, because yesterday disappeared before we knew what happened.

Mom and Granny and Sam and Michael and I were just finishing brunch when the doorbell rang this morning. I didn't care who was at the door. I just wanted to excuse myself from the table so I wouldn't have to hear Granny sing "Danny Boy" again. I thought Dad was ringing the doorbell, but it was Katie! She said she was going skating, and she asked me to go, too. She acted like nothing bad had happened between us, like we'd been hanging out together all along and I wasn't her enemy. At first I felt like telling Katie to take a hike. But I was so surprised and happy to see her, I said I'd go.

Katie didn't say a word all the way to the pond. She was humming and looking up at the sky, watching for snowflakes. So I didn't say anything, either. I whistled instead. We didn't even talk while we put on our skates. I took a few spins on the ice, but Katie was hanging back, along the edge of the pond. Then she tiptoed slowly onto the ice. And pretty soon she was circling me—and doing leaps and tucks and spins.

As long as I've known her, I've never ever seen Katie skate like she did today. For a while it was like she was out there all alone.

Then she glided slowly toward me and put out her hands to take hold of mine. We started spinning together, faster and faster. Pretty soon we were spinning so fast, we couldn't stay up straight. We both tumbled and went sliding on our butts across the ice. Katie and I were laughing so hard, my stomach ached and I couldn't breathe. Tears were streaming down my face, but they were the happy kind.

When we finally stopped laughing, we both lay there on the ice, gazing up at the sky and trying to catch snowflakes on our tongues. Then Katie started to cry for real. First she said she was sorry. Then she took hold of my hand and said, "Thank you, Fiona." She said it quietly, like she was dreaming, or maybe praying. I could feel my heart thumping, and for a minute I thought it might break—not from sorrow but because it was filled all the way up with joy.

I wanted to ask Katie if she was feeling better. I wanted to ask her about her secret diet, and about Victoria and her parents and John Robert. I wanted to ask her what she thinks about Mackenzie and whether she still likes Dylan. But I didn't ask Katie anything at all, except if she would come home with me for cocoa. And when she said yes, it finally felt like Christmas.

It felt even more like Christmas when Eliot stopped by this afternoon. He had a present for me, but I waited until now to open it. It's a copy of <u>Romeo and Juliet,</u> with a pretty cloth cover and a satin ribbon. Eliot had written on the very first page: *"For Fiona—O, she doth teach the torches to burn bright! Your Eliot."* <u>Thump-thump.</u> My heart is still pounding! I was glad I'd gotten Eliot a really nice blank book for his poems—and glad, too, that Natalie had done the lettering on the cover: *Poems and Other Magic.* And I'm especially glad that I saved my pretty valentine. It seems even more special now that I know Eliot made it for me.

I've had my very own secret admirer for months and months, but I didn't really realize it until today. Duh! Mom says that the best kind of love sneaks up on you when you're not looking. She sighed and said that falling in love with Dad was like being blasted from a deep sleep with fireworks and a 21-gun salute— and that was incredible. But with Michael, falling in love has been more like waking up slowly from a long, lazy nap and discovering that you're all snug and warm in a soft, lovely quilt.

Gunfire or a quilt? I don't think so. Knowing that Eliot likes me is somewhere in between!

Sunday, December 27

Katie and Blanca just called from Blanca's house.

The Hidalgos went to Los Angeles to spend Christmas with Blanca's aunt Isabel and uncle Sergio and their kids (including Alejandro). Katie was waiting on Blanca's front porch when the Hidalgos got home this afternoon. She wanted to talk with Blanca in private, just like she'd talked with me.

Blanca was squealing and laughing on the phone. I know

she's happy, too, because Katie seems more like...Katie. And I bet she's relieved, like I am, that John Robert is trying to help Katie and her parents figure out what's going on. Blanca wanted Katie and me to spend the night at her house tomorrow, but I'd already made plans to have Natalie sleep over. Now Blanca and Katie are coming here, too. Everybody is bringing her favorite movie, so we'll have a quadruple feature: Titanic (Blanca), Mermaids (Katie), The Princess Bride (Natalie), and Grease (me).

We'd better start popping corn and baking cookies and mulling cider now, because we'll be up until dawn watching all those movies!

Monday, December 28

Everybody is asleep, except me, and we barely even made it through Titanic.

Katie said she was nervous about sleeping over, but I'm glad she came. Mom and I have been reading a book about eating disorders. The book is interesting and a little scary. I guess there isn't exactly a cure for anorexia, but it's good that Katie feels stronger and has gained back two-and-a-half pounds. And at least tonight she ate a piece of pizza without chopping it all up. (She picked off all the pepperoni, but so did I!)

Last Saturday was the first day Katie had skated at all since she quit competing. She worried that she'd forgotten how. She said that at first she was so scared to skate again, she could barely stand up—but once she and I started spinning, it was more fun than she could ever remember having on the ice! She also said that when and if she competes again, she'd skate because she loves it, not because she needs a trophy to prove how good she is.

After we turned out the lights, Katie apologized to Blanca and me for the way she's treated us the past few months—and for the mean notes she wrote about both of us. Blanca started to ask Katie what she meant about the notes, but I said we should look ahead, not back, and Blanca and Katie agreed. (Blanca didn't know anything about that mean Blanca-is-like-the-Mississippi-River note, because I ripped it up before anybody else saw it. And I never knew for sure until today that Katie was the one who wrote that mean woodchuck note about me. Maybe she wanted to upset Blanca and me because she was feeling so lonely and scared and even sort of jealous.)

Then Katie told Natalie she was sorry for never giving her a chance—for deciding a year ago she didn't like her and never would. Katie said she'd worried for a long time that I'd forget about her if Natalie and I got to be good friends, especially because we're neighbors. Natalie told Katie, "Apology accepted." And Blanca and I both said, "Ditto!" Who could forget Katie?

Katie's mom called about five times tonight so Katie could sing and talk baby-talk to Victoria. She's the only person who can lull Victoria to sleep—and she's the only one who can make her laugh.

Katie still thinks Victoria Iris Larkin is a big poop, but now she wants to keep her!

Katie was the first one up this morning.

It was still dark out when she started tickling everybody, to wake us up. She said to hurry and get dressed because she had a surprise for us. Katie marched Blanca and Natalie and me down to the pond. Gully came, too. He's huge now, and he darts every which way, even on his leash! When we got to the south end of the pond, Katie scrambled to the top of a pile of dirt and pulled a little bottle out of her parka pocket. She stretched her arms wide and said, "Welcome, Spit Sisters, to New Babaloneya!" Then she opened the bottle, spit into it, and said, "I, <u>Zinnia</u> Spit, remain true to the Code of New Babaloneya: Truth, Honor, Friendship, <u>and Forgiveness</u>—No Matter What!" Katie passed the bottle to Blanca.

Blanca spit into it, too, and she said, "I, <u>Pansy</u> Spit, also remain true to the Code of New Babaloneya: Truth, Honor, Friendship, <u>and Forgiveness</u>—No Matter What!"

Then it was my turn to spit and proclaim: "I, <u>Daisy</u> Spit, remain true to the Code of New Babaloneya: Truth, Honor, Friendship... <u>and especially Forgiveness</u>—No Matter What!" When I handed the bottle to Natalie, she looked at me like I was crazy. She didn't know what to say, so I said: "Welcome to New Babaloneya, O gentle <u>Orchid</u> Spit!" (Orchid is the perfect New Babaloneyean name for Natalie, because she's so exotic and pretty.)

Natalie said, "Baloney stinks, but I love orchids!" And she spit into the bottle and promised to be true to the Code.

Gully stole the bottle from Natalie and ran off to bury it. We'll never find that bottle again, but it doesn't matter. We know it's out there somewhere, just like the bottle that Blanca, Katie, and I buried years ago in the backyard on Orchard Lane.

The sky was glowing bright pink and yellow by the time we got home this morning—the Spit Sisters holding hands, all four of us happy and hungry for the cinnamon rolls we could smell baking in Mom's cozy kitchen.

Wednesday, December 30

Katie stopped by Mom's early this morning to go skating again.

We went down to the pond, but we never did skate. The bulldozers were making lots of noise, digging and pushing dirt around. So we just sat on a big log and watched for a long time. Then Katie started to talk—she was whispering, really—about what it's like for her to be hungry. She said that for the longest time, being hungry was the one thing she could count on. It's like the hole gnawing away inside of her filled her up somehow, so she could almost forget about other stuff that worried her—like her parents being too busy and preoccupied to really listen to her.

At first nothing Katie said made sense. How can a hole fill you up? But the more she talked, the more I remembered what it was like when Mom and Dad were getting divorced. Everything seemed scary and awful. And after a while, being scared began to feel almost normal—I didn't want to laugh, or even to try to have fun. That doesn't make a lot of sense now, but it's how I felt. And I guess Katie felt that even though she wasn't sure what would happen when the baby was born or what her parents would think if she quit skating competitively, she knew just how she would feel if she skipped a meal or two or three. And she knew exactly how she would feel if she ate a bowl of dry cornflakes or a piece of plain chicken. Eating was the one thing in her life that Katie was the boss of.

I told Katie that I've always envied her because everything about her seems perfect. She laughed, like that was a joke. But it's true: For as long as I can remember, Katie's life has always looked just right—her house, her parents, her clothes and hair, and even her thin body. It turns out that all the time I was envying Katie, she was envying me, too, because I have Sam, and parents who used to let us roller-skate around the kitchen. But Katie didn't know that Mom and Dad also used to fight like wild cats when they weren't roller-skating with us. And I didn't know that Katie's parents made her dress up and play dreary Chopin music with them every single night after dinner. I guess almost every family has secrets, and some of them aren't too fun.

Katie asked for Miss Dupré's address. She never really liked Miss Dupré—she even transferred out of her Language Arts class in sixth grade because it seemed too busy and strange and personal to her. But Mrs. Larkin told Katie that Miss Dupré has been concerned about her, and how she was involved, all the way from New Orleans, in helping Katie. So Katie wants to write to her, to thank her and to tell her she's doing better.

I wanted to ask Katie about her strange haircut, but it didn't seem like the right moment!

Thursday, December 31

Another year—gone!

Was it good or bad? Probably some of both, like every year—but it was definitely <u>interesting.</u> The worst part was worrying about Katie for months and months. And the best part was this past week, knowing that Katie is starting to feel stronger and a little happier. Miss Dupré going back to New Orleans was bad, but she's still as close as the stars in the sky—and the telescope and telephone! Besides, Mr. Riddle eventually took her place, and he's a great teacher, too. (Even Ms. Smoot ended up being OK.) Simon turned out to be pond scum, but if I was still wasting my time on Simon James, I'd never have realized that Eliot S. Thomas is awesome!

Even though Mackenzie Swanson is BAD NEWS, Mom thinks that trying to understand her better might be a good resolution for me for next year. <u>No way!</u> Figuring out whether Mackenzie is going to be nice or mean (depending on what she wants from me) takes way too much energy. Besides, I've got more important things to think about in the year ahead—like the bulldozers tearing up the pond to build all those condos. And Mom and Michael. And Granny Ryan maybe coming to live with us.

Who knows what the New Year will bring? I don't even know for sure what's going to happen tonight, except that all of us—

Granny, Sam, Mom, and Michael, plus Mama and Papa Jardin and Uncle Harvey and Dad, and me—are meeting the Hidalgos and the Larkins at the pond for a skating party, just like old times. And Eliot's family is coming, too, to add a new twist!

Will Eliot hold my hand when we skate? What if there's mistletoe and he tries to kiss me? What if there's mistletoe and he doesn't? Maybe I, Fiona Claire Jardin, will have to kiss Eliot S. Thomas if he doesn't kiss me.

What does that S. stand for, anyway?

ACKNOWLEDGMENTS

It's no accident that friendship is at the heart of the second installment of Fiona's adventures and journals. The subject has intrigued me since... well, since before I was born.

I'm convinced that as a twin I got a jump, in utero, on experiencing the alchemy that turns two distinct individuals into close friends. And unlike most toddlers, I understood all too well that I alone was *not* the center of the universe. My twin brother, John Robert, and I were prewired to share almost everything, side-by-side. And perhaps as a result, even as toddlers we also got a glimmer of the generosity of spirit that graces every true friendship.

Unlike Fiona, who at the age of twelve begins to understand just how magical friendship can be, I have been slow to truly appreciate how blessed I have been in terms of the friends who illuminate my life. It's been more than three decades since we cavorted and, yes, quarreled together on a daily basis, but even today I remain in close touch with not only my twin brother but also our older sisters, Shauneen and Kathleen, as well as with several pals from our childhood and adolescence in Falls Church, Virginia. I likewise cherish more than a few friendships that date back to my college daze in Middlebury, Vermont, and to the impossibly hopeful (not to mention sleep-deprived) early years of marriage and young parenthood in Denver, Colorado.

The friendships I have forged during the past decade in Southern California are no less precious to me. Heartfelt thanks to the constellation of remarkable women who for years gathered to write, to talk, and to laugh and cry around my kitchen table, and to my stellar colleagues at Harcourt, especially the indefatigable Allyn Johnston.

I trust that each of you knows, without my signaling you by name, just how profoundly you have touched my life. *Fiona's Private Pages* is my small bouquet of gratitude and love to all of you, and most especially to the finest friends of all—my children, Andrew Stewart Bayer, Henry Eliot Bayer, and Hannah Caitlin Bayer.

R. C.

January 2000

For John Robert, my twin and lifelong friend
For Michaels, one and all
And for True Friends everywhere...

Copyright © 2000 by Roberta Ann Cruise

www.HarcourtBooks.com

First Harcourt Paperbacks edition 2002

Library of Congress Cataloging-in-Publication Data
Cruise, Robin, 1951–
Fiona's private pages/Robin Cruise.
p. cm.
Summary: Eleven-year-old Fiona describes her triumphs and struggles with
friendship in her very private journal.
[1. Friendship—Fiction. 2. Diaries—Fiction.] I. Title.
PZ7.C88828Fi 2000
[Fic]—dc21 99-50559
ISBN 0-15-202210-4
ISBN 0-15-216572-X pb

Text set in Clearface
Display type hand-lettered by Robin Cruise
Designed by Kaelin Chappell

A C E G H F D B

With special thanks to Erin Trimble, Jessica Fulton, and Amy Baker,
for putting a little pizzazz on the front cover, and to Hannah Caitlin Bayer,
for lending some of her junk!
—R. C.

Each friend represents a world in us,
a world possibly not born until they arrive,
and it is only by this meeting
that a new world is born.

—Anaïs Nin